Thank you so much for having me!

Detached
Book 1 of the Fleischer Series

4th Edition

Wendi L. Starusnak

WENDI STARUSNAK

DEDICATION

I'd like to dedicate Detached to my loving husband Ron and all of our exceptional children (Ashley, Ronnie, David, Jade, Derrick, Jenna, Laurie, and Luke) who never gave up on me, continued to encourage me even when I felt like there was nothing to encourage, and dealt with me through the emotional roller-coaster I seemed to ride while writing this novel. Without them, Detached would never have been written. Thank you and I love you all!

NOTE FROM THE AUTHOR

Detached is a work of fiction. It's not true. There are truths woven throughout, some mine, some belonging to others, and some are just made up. Do things like what happened in Detached really happen? Yes, unfortunately they do. The main message in Detached is that abuse is a vicious cycle. This will be the main message in Book 2 of the Fleischer Series as well. You see, abuse feeds on silence and ignorance. Sweep it under the carpet, pretend it doesn't happen, that it's not as bad as it seems or that it could be worse. Pretend that it's not your problem. This is what abuse hungers for, what it needs to continue to haunt little children and grown adults alike. This is how abuse recruits its followers, it creates monsters out of once-beautiful people by putting them through unspeakable torments.

I urge everyone to find their voice, to speak out against abuse when you see it or suspect it, or when it happens to you. Do what that little voice in your heart is begging you to do. It may not be the easy thing to do, anything worth doing rarely is, but it's the right thing to do. And remember: Abuse feeds on silence and ignorance.

DISCLAIMER

ACKNOWLEDGMENTS

Tasha Gwartney- for an amazing cover,
Susan Lynch- for a professional editing job,
Bryan Airel- for the best proofreading job I could have asked for,
Andrea Smith- for great feedback and proofreading,
Christine Vorndran and Louis Neverette, for always being there for
me,
All the amazing ladies (especially Noreen, Bonnie, and Sue) at my
Writer's Workshop for the help, encouragement and praise along the
way,
Grandma Cron for her input and encouragement and for living a life
worthy of a hundred best sellers,
Mom & Dad for reading my manuscript and giving me honest
feedback and advice,
My brother Robbie for his support and input,
The SWAT Team for not confiscating my computer during that last
raid,
&
Aunt Ginny (Virginia Buffett) for the "Don't get too attached
because it might be supper" idea and phrase.
I give you all my sincere gratitude. I'm truly sorry if I've left anyone
out. There are so many people that have given me advice,
encouragement, and believed in me along my journey that I couldn't
possibly mention all of them here.

CHAPTER ONE

I felt the back of his rough, calloused hand slam into the side of my face. My whole head jerked around with the force and I had to grab the counter to keep from falling to the cold, hardwood floor. "Don't cry. Don't give him the satisfaction," that voice in my head said, the one that was always there that I didn't recognize as my own. The voice was that of my doll, Julie.

Dad turned to face the rest of our family again. "I don't want none of you belly achin' over that dumb horse. It had ta be done. Tha's all. Yer all lucky I din' make one of you do it. Don't I always tell ya, don't git too attached 'cuz it might be supper? I think some of you haven't been paying enough attention to me when I speak. Maybe now my message is clear enough for all of you. Now go and get ready fer bed," Dad said in that stupid fake accent he always seemed to use for some reason whenever he was angry. That thought was forgotten about as fast as it had come when Dad spit his tobacco into one of the three dirty cups that remained on the counter. I had to stop myself from gagging at the idea of his blob of goobery, stinky spit just sitting in a brown pool at the bottom of the cup.

My heart ached along with my face. It was stupid of me to question him. I would have to remember to keep my big mouth shut before it got me seriously hurt. "You know it doesn't do any good trying to reason with that guy," said Julie's voice again. There was something warm and thick trickling down my lip. I knew from experience that I must be bleeding. I licked the blood off the side of my split lip with my tongue as I told myself that she was right.

We all knew Dad's words well, "Don't get too attached because it might be supper," or some version of that. He had never used those words to explain feeding us our pet horse or anything of that sort. The first time I had ever heard him say that was when I was about five or six years old and one of our pigs had babies. I wanted to keep one for a pet. They had been so adorable and I hated to think they would only grow up and get fat so that we could cut them up to eat them. I ended up getting a beating because I couldn't stop myself from crying.

I was careful to keep my gaze focused on the plate I was washing to avoid eye contact with any of my siblings or either of my parents. There was a crack in the plate, right down the center, but the plate didn't break. The crack had been there for a while, through several washings. Printed on the back were the words 'Syracuse China'. Strangely, I found new strength in the cracked plate that refused to break. My family was a lot like this plate. "That's enough. You don't want to cry and get yourself into more trouble," said Julie's sensible voice from my head. Finally I heard them push their chairs away from the dinner table.

There was a sniffle from behind me. Without thinking, I turned my head and saw the disgusted look on Johnny's face. He noticed me look at him and quickly fixed the expression on his face so as to try not to give away his all too obvious emotions. I was heartbroken for my older brother as well as for the rest of my family.

I hated my father. I hated him before he fed us Whisper, our beautiful mare, and I hated him even more now. I would forever despise that disgusting beast. But I didn't dare say that out loud. I didn't even dare to think it where he could see me. So I turned my head again, trying to stay as invisible as possible while I finished up washing the last of the dishes.

Our dish drainer had rusted and been thrown out several

months before now. My parents hadn't bothered to buy a new one yet so I just set the dishes carefully on a towel on the counter until I was ready to dry and put them away.

In my mind I could still hear Whisper as she whinnied in happiness while I groomed her beautiful blonde mane only the day before yesterday. She had looked at me with one of those big brown eyes and seemed to understand my troubles as I poured the contents of my aching heart out to her.

Then I had taken her for a run to give her some exercise. I could still feel Whisper's raw strength beneath me as I pushed her to run faster along the side of the almost deserted gravel road. There wasn't another house for probably a mile, just open fields and trees. I hadn't wanted her to stop ever. I wanted to ride off to someplace unknown, away from my father and the horrible things that he did, and live happily ever after, like they always seemed to do in the fairytales that I read.

But instead, Whisper and I had made the short journey along the gravel road back to our yellow, two story farmhouse that looked so nice and normal from the outside. We journeyed slowly past our produce stand that was in desperate need of a new coat of brown paint for the season and up the slightly curved dirt driveway.

In the late summer and early fall I liked to pick two apples off from one of the trees on our way up the driveway. I would give one to Whisper as a treat and keep one to snack on myself. The first crunch through the crisp skin as the juice from inside squirted out and into my dry mouth was a memory that always made me look forward to the end of summer. It wasn't apple season yet though. So the six apple trees that we had lining the left side of the driveway weren't yet producing apples. I realized that I wouldn't be able to feed one to Whisper this year or ever again.

I jumped to the ground and led Whisper by the reins around the large, open front porch of our house. Two brown rocking chairs sat there, empty as usual, with a matching round end table between them that would look just right with a sweating pitcher of lemonade and two glasses sitting on it. I could remember Mom sitting in one of those rocking chairs and reading a book when I was younger, keeping an eye on the four of us kids as we played together in the front yard. Eric could barely walk then. It had been a long time since I had seen either of my parents sitting out on our front porch for any reason. That was such a shame. There was something kind of peaceful about my parents sitting on the porch just talking and watching us kids play.

We walked past the big brown barn and the noisy chickens to the fenced area of grass where we kept the horses. There were only two: Whisper, our pet, and Buster, our work horse. Whisper's leg had been injured as a foal and she wasn't able to pull heavy loads the way that Buster could. The only reason Dad allowed her to stay around was so that us kids could learn how to ride on her.

I couldn't help but think that if we had not come home that day, she would still be here with us now. I couldn't throw up. Or cry. But Whisper was gone. And gone to... I couldn't even bear the thought of where she had gone to without my dinner trying to come back up. My mouth got that horrible watery feeling and then I started to gag on the thoughts that were catching in the back of my throat. I was sick to my stomach with disgust and grief, but I was terrified of Dad and what more he would do. "He'll know if you get sick and then things will end up being even worse. Stop thinking about it," I heard Julie say in my head. I wanted to wash my mouth to get the taste of Whisper out of it.

I'm sure he wanted more than anything for one of us to stomp or drag our feet. Then he would have an excuse to let loose on one or more of us. We all knew better. And we all needed time to heal from the horrible loss of our beloved pet before being put through any more pain.

I made the hike to the room I shared with my younger sister Caroline, keeping in mind the fact that Dad was probably watching our movements for anything not quite right. Johnny and our youngest sibling Eric were already ahead of me on the way upstairs to their room, right across the narrow hallway from ours.

Our rooms were actually in the attic, but it was all finished and insulated with sheet rocked walls and ceilings. The ceilings were also slanted because we were just under the roof, so my side of the room was on the taller side as was Johnny's in the boy's room.

It was gloomy looking and dusty smelling up here, but not much more than the rest of the house was. In the winter it was a little colder up here than downstairs, and in the summer it was normally always hotter and stuffier- often it was almost too stuffy to breathe. Sometimes it felt as if the walls of the room would close right in on us. In the same way that our bedrooms didn't really belong in this house, a lot of times I felt as if I didn't truly belong anywhere in this world and most of the time I actually welcomed the suffocating feeling.

Caroline, my younger sister, was right behind me with our goofy mutt, Lucky. He had black and gray fur that was a little wavy when it got long and he wasn't any bigger than a fully grown cat would be. My father normally shaved his fur off once in the Spring to help get rid of any fleas and to help keep Lucky cooler for the Summer. I didn't really think it did much for the fleas, but it probably did work to make him cooler. In fact, it was probably already time for my father to shave him again.

I wondered whose idea had it been to give a dog of ours a name like Lucky? Why was he lucky? Lucky he was brought home by us instead of being out on his own? No chores to do, nobody to answer to, no rules to follow? Free to do whatever. That all actually sounded so peaceful and relaxing.

The thought of being free was so strange to me. It felt like I was just another one of my father's slaves. Everything we did was carefully watched by him: the way we sat, the way we ate our food, the way that we acted with each other and with strangers, even the way that we did our chores. We were never free. Even when we managed to sleep through the night without him sneaking into one of our rooms, he managed to haunt my dreams and probably the dreams of the rest of my family as well.

Freedom sounded like a good title for a story that I could write. Yes! I could write a story like that tomorrow, maybe after our normal school lessons instead of reading. I always wrote down stories as soon as I got the chance after an idea popped into my head. Sometimes an idea for a good story came to me twice in one week and sometimes it was months before I had anything that I felt was worth being written down.

Mom normally gave us a little extra time after our regular schoolwork to read or write whatever we wanted. She said that you could go anywhere you wanted in a good book and be whoever you wanted. I agreed with her and had many great adventures while reading different books that Mom had saved from her mother and from her own childhood. I read whenever I got the chance, normally after our school lessons and just before bed, and finished about one book each week. Reading the books that I knew my mother had once read also made me feel closer to her, like we had somehow shared the experiences that took place among the pages.

Reading and writing were just about the only times that I ever felt anything close to peace. It was my only escape from the constant fear and worry that was my life. Well, that and the rare times that we kids all got to spend time just playing together.

I listened for our door to latch before deciding on which nightgown to wear for bed. It was Spring and getting warmer every day, but there was always a dampness in this house that caused a constant feeling of being chilled to the bone. For that reason, among others, I wanted to wear the pajamas that left the least amount of my skin showing. After noting the familiar click, I went to our dresser and fought with the top drawer until it finally pried free.

I couldn't remember a time when I didn't have to struggle to open the drawers on our dresser. It was old and Mom said it was an antique, like much of our furniture was, our dresser having been hers when she was a little girl. I took out my pink cotton nightgown, the longest one I had. I slipped it over my head and it fell to just below my knees. My hair got all staticky and I ran my hands over it to calm it back down. "Will you get mine for me too, Emily?"

"Sure." As I was wrestling with the drawer once more and thinking about what my mother must have been like as a little girl, I heard commotion coming from downstairs.

"Why would you do that, you stupid fuckin' bitch," I heard Dad shout. Then I heard the sharp crack of skin making hard contact with other skin, followed by more shouting from Dad, "I don't know why I keep fucking putting up with your bullshit! You're nothing but a lazy goddamned cunt, no better than those inbred kids of ours!"

Huh? What did he mean by that? Mom was screaming, "I'm sorry," over and over and crying. Hot, salty tasting tears started making their way from my eyes to my nose and down onto my hands. My nose started to run and my face felt like it would burst into angry flames.

I didn't want my mom to get hurt, but at the same time Julie was telling me in my head, "It's better than one of you getting beat. I actually hope that he wears himself out with her and leaves the rest of you alone for the night." I made up my mind while drying my face that I wasn't going to worry about what was taking place downstairs. Focusing my attention on the dresser once more, I yanked on the drawer I had been fighting with, this time with more force. It still wasn't budging.

I had to make sure that Caroline didn't do something to accidentally to draw unwanted attention to us. Turning my head to glance at my sister, I noticed her big blue eyes were wide with worry. She caught me looking at her and began to sob. Lucky seemed to know she needed comfort and jumped onto her lap to lick the tears away from her face. I decided I could continue my struggle with the dresser drawer another time.

I wished I could make everything all better for my little sister, but I couldn't. Maybe I could at least take her mind off of things for a little while by telling her a nice story. So I grabbed my doll Julie off from my pillow (I didn't want Julie to get jealous or upset with me for not paying enough attention to her) and went to Caroline's bed,

14

wrapped my arms around her and began spinning a wonderful tale about a little girl who ended up in a beautiful world made of all sorts of candy. I had written a story like it during our free reading and writing time about a month ago. So far it was my favorite out of all the stories I had written.

"And there she stayed and lived happily ever after," I felt her breathing on my bare arm become more steady and her body go limp. I laid her head on her pillow (boy, she was pretty heavy!) and pulled her covers up over her shoulders.

I decided to leave Lucky lying above the blankets at her feet. He was only a small dog anyways. I didn't know why he wasn't allowed on the furniture. It wasn't like our furniture was all that great. Most of it was really old and worn out, and Lucky was a part of our family. At least I thought so. I loved him and I know he loved us too. He seemed to feel our sadness, worry, get excited to see us, and anything else that a loving member of a family should do. Of course, that was how I had felt about Whisper too. I was pretty sure now that Dad hadn't felt the same way.

I'm Julie. I'm more than just Emily's doll or the voice in her head that she doesn't even recognize. I'm a part of her. I've seen things, things that Emily doesn't even realize have happened or do happen. Her problem is that she lets her emotions get in the way too much. I don't have that problem. I still can't believe that heartless bastard killed their horse. I knew he was no good. I didn't realize just how rotten he could be, I guess. The horse is in a better place now at least, anywhere is probably better than here with that man in charge. Someday I'll get my turn to take care of things. Then everything will be different.

CHAPTER TWO

I felt kind of responsible for Caroline since I was her older sister and all. The problem was that I was still only a girl myself and no match for the evil human being that we were unlucky enough to be born to. I was satisfied and relieved that I was able to set her mind free from this place, from being a member of the Fleischer family, if only for a short while. Caroline was still dressed in her clothes from the day and the dog was where he didn't belong but, if there really was a God, no one would be coming into our room tonight to know the difference.

She looked so peaceful lying there. Her beautiful long, thick brown hair sprawled out around her head, covering the pillow. She always cried as it was being brushed. My mother always threatened to cut it off, but my father wouldn't allow that. So Caroline practiced brushing her own hair every day, probably hoping that she would be able to do it on her own soon.

She took more after Mom with her looks and was a bit on the chubby side. My parents both said it was just her baby fat and she would slim down as she grew older. I wondered about that. I had always been skinny.

Either way, Caroline was still beautiful. She was only eight years old, a whole three years younger than me, and that alone made the things that our father did so much worse for her. She was more emotional than I was too; probably because she was still so young.

She would learn in time to hide her feelings, at least from Dad. I was still working on learning that lesson myself. The best I could do to protect her was to help teach her when it was wise to stay quiet and out of the way (which was most of the time).

I always worried about my brothers and my sister. All the time. How could I care so much about them, yet our parents seem to care so little? How could my father do such horrible things and still tell himself that he loved us? Did he even tell himself that he loved us? He acted like he hated every single one of us. I didn't know for sure if he did the same kind of horrible nasty things to the boys as he did to us girls because we never talked about it. But there were many small clues that he had, besides the fact that all of us avoided spending any time alone with him.

My older brother Johnny was fourteen. I hoped and prayed that when he got big enough one day he would save all of us. He was bigger than Mom already and almost as big as Dad, but not quite. And not as strong yet either. He was skinny too, like me, but not puny. You could tell he had muscles from working on our farm just by looking at him.

Over this past year his voice had changed from a little boy's voice to more of a man's voice. His looks had changed too, losing that little boy quality. Now his nose appeared narrower and his chin more defined, along with his Adam's apple. At least that's what my mother had called it. Like God had taken a chisel and chipped away at my older brother until all the little boy that was left of him was gone. He had dark hair, almost black, with just a little blonde patch at his part in the front. That, along with his bright blue eyes, would make him quite the heart breaker Mom had said. Just like our father, that's what she said.

I had to admit that Johnny did take after Dad with his looks, but his personality made him appear completely different than our father did to me. I thought Johnny was actually pretty handsome. But I was a little confused about the heart breaker bit. Why did he have to break hearts at all? Maybe he would find the one girl that was right for him and nobody's heart would have to get broken. Maybe he didn't even want a girl at all ever and that would be fine too.

Johnny was stubborn and I knew the beatings Dad gave him were hard on him. He barely complained and only cried when he thought he was alone and no one could hear him. But sometimes I did.

He didn't play anymore like the rest of us still liked to when we got the chance. That had changed over this past year also. Johnny seemed to enjoy being alone. Mostly fishing.

Maybe our big brother was making plans to save us. Or (and I hoped I was wrong about this one), maybe instead of saving us, Johnny was making plans to leave us behind. Sometimes that voice in my head tried to tell me that. I refused to believe it. Johnny and I used to be so close, being the oldest of the kids. I still liked to think that we were, just we were both getting older.

Eric was my younger brother, seven years old. He was a trouble maker, loud and always busy, busy, busy. And he was a little slow, like with his talking and his thinking. We had to explain everything to Eric, often two or three times. I sometimes got frustrated with my little brother, but I loved him. His childishness was so adorable and I just felt like hiding him from the world and all of its pain.

Eric was pudgier too, like Caroline and my mother. It was cute on him. He had freckles and his front teeth looked too big for his mouth. His hair was thin like mine and he was a red head.

I wondered how we all ended up looking so different but also so much alike. I thought it was funny how that all worked. Mom told us that it was because Dad had black hair and she had blonde. Sometimes you ended up with a little of everything in between.

Mom wasn't much help at all where Dad was concerned. I think she was just as afraid of Dad and seemed just as stuck in the nightmare as we were. Most of the time lately I think she was just too drunk to care anyways.

Mom was a lot smaller than Dad was, not skinny-wise (he told her all the time how fat she was and ugly too, but I didn't think so), but height-wise. She was only a little taller than me now. When we both stood face to face my eyes were even with her nose. I didn't think she was beautiful, but she definitely wasn't ugly either. My mother was just ordinary. I thought ordinary was good. It seemed to be less noticeable.

I often wondered if other people could see how sad she was just by looking at her. I thought I could. Sometimes I would look at her and swear the skin on her face was drooping. It probably was from being so sad all the time. I would be sad if I was stuck married to such a miserable man. And I didn't think she even knew yet how truly horrible he really was to us kids.

She told me once that Dad had a rough childhood full of hurt and he swore he would never be the weak little boy that he once was again. Maybe he told himself that he was teaching us to be tough. I tried not to hate him, I really did. But there was nothing nice to say about him. There was nothing nice that I could ever think of to say anyhow.

Mom talked to me sometimes about things, but not very often. I treasured the time that we spent together like that. I especially enjoyed it when she wasn't drinking. I just had to be careful to listen to what she had to say and not ask too many of my own questions because sometimes that made her stop talking right away.

Most of the time my mother was teaching me a new chore when she talked to me. I couldn't think of any chores I still had left to learn though. So our talks were a lot less often and would probably slowly come to a stop in the years to come. That realization made me a little sad.

The first thing I could clearly remember being taught by my mother was how and what to dust. And that you should dust before doing any of the other cleaning chores in the same room, otherwise all of the cleaning that had been done before the dusting would have to be done again. Mom had said, "To explain what I mean: you wouldn't want to dust the coffee table and then sweep the cobwebs from the ceiling. Then you would just end up with a bunch of dust and cobwebs on the coffee table and have to dust that all over again." She had also talked to me about the day I was born during that lesson.

She told me as we dusted the nick-knacks about how her water had broken just before noon on a dreary, drizzly Saturday morning, the 18th of July in 1964. She had been outside getting vegetables from the garden to go along with that night's dinner. The contractions came on hard and strong after that and she made her way slowly to the barn where she knew my father was piling hay. She and my father were both worried that they would never make it to the hospital in time. They didn't even make it into the house. She gave birth to me right there in the barn. She told me how they both fell in love with me the minute they saw me. I loved that story and liked to think maybe at that point my father wasn't such a bad man. It was by far one of the best memories I had of any of my mother's talks with me.

There were more talks on different subjects throughout the years as I learned how to wash dishes from start to finish, how to wash laundry, by hand when necessary and in the machine, and also how to hang it out to dry.

While teaching me to hang clothes on the line she told me a story that her mother used to tell her. If nightfall came and the clothes were still left hanging out on the line, my grandmother had told my mother that restless spirits would be able to put the clothes on and wear them themselves. Then they would be free to roam the earth as any living person would for the entire night. She told my mom that sometimes the spirits didn't even bother hanging the clothes back up, just left them lying on the ground. Also, the clothes that were worn by the restless spirits were always more stiff than the rest, because some of the 'dead' had stayed in them.

My mother told me that she never really believed the story, but thought that it was just an imaginative way to get her to remember not to leave the clothes out on the line too long. I never planned to leave the clothes out on the line long enough to find out for myself.

Then she had taught me how to iron, what to iron, what to hang and what and how to fold. From what I could tell, everything got ironed and most things got hung, except pajamas and underwear, which got folded neatly after being ironed. I didn't really understand the point of ironing the underwear, but I would do as I was taught.

She told me stories as she gradually taught me all the basics of cooking. Mom always told me during my cooking lessons that as long as I knew the basics, the only thing left was to have a good recipe to follow. She also taught me that being able to cook was the key to finding a good man and that good food was the key to a happy family. I thought she must have had blinders to her own husband and family on if she thought that was true. I found that I was actually pretty darn good at cooking though and I really enjoyed it.

There were other chores and more stories and talks, like gathering the fresh fruits and vegetables from outside, making the beds, mending clothing, sewing new clothing, and so on. I enjoyed all of it.

I didn't know if we had any other living family. Like grandparents, uncles, aunts, cousins, or anything else. We pretty much kept to ourselves. I did know that my father's parents had both died in a tragic accident when he was only seventeen years old. That's how we ended up with our house and the land that it was on. Dad had inherited it when his parents passed away. But that was all that I knew. I didn't know what the tragic accident was, how old my grandparents were at the time, or anything else.

Sometimes I dreamed of what my grandparents would have been like or what it would be like to play Hide and Seek with a bunch of cousins. I also dreamed of having a rich aunt that adored me and spoiled me that decided to take me away on a fantastic adventure with her. But, besides my mother telling me little stories here and there about her own childhood, our parents always skirted the issue of other family and we had none that I knew of. So there were never any big family gatherings where we brought a salad or baked beans to pass around like there were in some of the books that I read.

No one ever came to visit us either, except for the people that stopped by the produce stand in our front lawn to buy food from us. Sometimes Dad took one or two of us kids with him when he went into town to buy stuff that we needed. But Dad had always taught us that kids are supposed to be "seen and not heard", so none of us ever really got a chance to get to know anybody.

We didn't go to school either like a lot of other kids did. We were home-schooled. That's what Mom and Dad called it. We sure did learn a lot of things at home. A little bit of brain work each day and a whole lot of chores around the house and farm. That counted as school for us.

Occasionally, we worked on some math, spelling, reading, geography, history, and science. Mostly we learned stuff that was related to living life, paying bills, keeping house and farming. The boys did chores like mowing the lawn, cleaning the barn and fenced animal areas, feeding the animals, milking the cows, helping with butchering and cleaning dinner, plowing and planting the fields for crops, fishing, burning the garbage that was able to be burned, and so on.

Caroline and I helped with everything around the house and a little of the outside stuff also. We gathered eggs, groomed the animals, sometimes helped when it was time to plant the crops, gathered fresh vegetables and fruit from the field for our meals, and picked berries when they were ripe. We helped prepare and cook meals, washed dishes, did laundry, dusted and cleaned around the house, mended clothing, sewed, and anything else that was considered woman's work. I did more than Caroline, of course, because I was older.

Mom had told me too that the State considered all of these little chores that we did to be some sort of school work. We got school credit for everything that we learned and everything that we did.

Mom also said that someone from the State could come to check up on us at any time to make sure that we could really do everything that she wrote down.

We already took two written tests a year for the State, but those tests were only on Math, Science, English, and Social Studies. According to Mom, the State said that I was reading and writing at a high school level, which she seemed very proud of. She said I was great in the other things she taught me as well and we would be fine if the State ever did come to double check on things.

I wondered how many other kids got home-schooled like us. I thought about that and decided that if other kids were taught at home it must be because their parents had something they wanted kept hidden just like my father did. What other reason would someone have not to send their children to regular school?

Then I wondered if even some of the kids in the big schools got Sex Education too, the way that we did first hand from our father. I knew that there was such a thing as Sex Education, because Johnny had a textbook he had to do work from on the subject. Just thinking or reading about the word "sex" made me nervous and want to hide under my covers. I sure would like to think that not all kids had to feel that way.

Our parents said that we didn't need or want anyone else in our lives. They said that we were all that each other would ever need. I hoped and prayed almost every day for more.

I lifted Julie off Caroline's bed with care, as if she were a real baby. She was about a foot and a half long and her skin was made of rubber, except for the eyes. Those were made of plastic. Her eyelids closed and opened, depending on how she was positioned. I had written the name I gave her on her buttocks in ink so that it wouldn't wear off easily. Her hair was a little curly and light brown like mine was and her eyes were brown.

I really did love my doll, but I was afraid of her as well. There seemed to be something hiding behind her eyes, something that reminded me too much of a real person with real feelings.

Sometimes I actually even believed that maybe Julie was the other voice that I sometimes heard in my head, but I knew that was just my active imagination. I called the other voice Julie anyways, just because it seemed to fit.

I was worried that Julie might come alive in the night or when no one was watching and do evil things. I knew I was more than a little crazy for thinking like that, but it was how I felt. Sometimes I had these images flash in my mind of her doing something really bad, like holding a little knife and chasing after somebody. That's why I was always extra kind and loving to her. So if Julie really did come to life maybe she would remember how good I was to her and, in return, not hurt me.

I laid Julie on my pillow then turned out the light and climbed into bed. I made sure as I did that my nightgown stayed where it belonged by holding it in place with my left hand. Then I lifted the covers over myself, again holding my nightgown down so it didn't move. I positioned Julie in my arms so that I would wake up if she moved at all while I was asleep, like I did every night. "There, now you're all comfy," I said cheerfully to her.

Then I whispered my favorite bedtime prayer, sure that God would answer when the time was right. "Now I lay me down to sleep. I pray You Lord my soul to keep. And if I should escape before I awake, I pray You Lord my soul to take. Amen." It wasn't long before I began to drift off to sleep with Julie in my arms.

That was quite surprising for a girl like Emily who had so much on her mind. Sometimes it took Emily a long time to go to sleep and then other nights she seemed to fall asleep as soon as her head hit the pillow. I could stay awake all night if I wanted. I rested when the risk for danger seemed to be low. Otherwise I stayed alert and ready for whatever I might need to handle. So far Emily hadn't wanted me to handle anything, but someday she wouldn't be able to stop me anymore. She didn't really understand yet about me or who I am, but someday she will realize that I'm stronger than her and that I'm only here to help her.

CHAPTER THREE

I woke up, left Julie lying on my pillow, and went immediately to the window to try to see what time of day it might be. I moved the heavy cloth curtain out of the way, making more of that little dust that always seemed to float around in the air even though we were constantly dusting and cleaning everything. I squinted to try to see better through the window, that foggy stuff that collected between the panes for years making it almost impossible to see through clearly. It must be sometime in the early morning hours, because it looked as if the sun were just getting out of bed itself. Good. That meant that we had no late night visitors during the dark hours.

I needed to wake Caroline up and have her get dressed in the new day's clothes before someone found out that she had never changed last night. I hated to wake her. She seemed to be sleeping so well for once. No bad dreams had disturbed her sleep as far as I could tell and no real life nightmares had either.

I wasn't afraid of monsters hiding under my bed, not the way that everyone else thinks of them anyhow. I often had the same nightmare on different nights about our father hiding under my bed. He was scarier than anything else that I could have ever imagined on my own.

In these nightmares he would hide there under the bed on the splintery wood floor just until I had fallen nicely asleep. Then when I was no longer on guard he would peek his head out and slowly reach his arm up. He would grab one of my ankles and then drag me off from my bed, blankets and all. I would hit the floor hard with my shoulder blades and my head. Huge splinters from the floor jabbed into the bare skin on my back and thighs. They would bury themselves there as my father pulled me under the bed with him.

Only in my nightmare, under the bed wasn't under the bed anymore. It was some dark, creepy, wet forest floor. I normally ended up waking up by that point; my heart racing and checking myself for the splinters that I swore must be bulging from underneath my skin.

I realized that I had been just standing there staring into space when I was snapped back to the present by sounds in the hallway. I heard my father's heavy, slow footsteps as they began to approach our closed door. I was frozen by fear and an undeniable urge to hide. I could see his worn, brown, leather boots with a hole starting to form near the big toe on his right boot walking carefully toward our door in my mind.

God, please don't let him come in here! What does he want anyways? "The bed! Maybe he'll think you're both still sleeping and just go away," said Julie's voice in my head. I climbed back under my covers as quickly as I could without making so much as a sound. I noticed the bed was still warm where I had been laying before I got up.

I laid there doing my best to look like I was still asleep. I shushed Julie, just in case, who was lying next to me. I had to remember to relax, breathe slowly, and not scrunch my eyes shut. As soon as I had my eyes closed, I heard the knob on the door being turned and the door open.

God, please don't let something bad happen. Please, please, please. I heard the familiar click as our door closed and then the sound of his footsteps headed between our beds. His presence cast a shadow over my closed lids. Then I heard my sister moan in her sleep and I knew he was the one disturbing her. Oh no! Please don't let him bother her. Not with me right here to have to witness it. I had to do something. I couldn't just lay here and let that happen.

"Dammit," he said to himself, just as I was about to cough and pretend to wake up. Ah, she still had her clothes on. I guess that was more work than he was willing to take on just then. I cringed as I heard Lucky yelp after being whacked in his muzzle and then jump down off the bed.

"Now is a good time to wake up, before he decides to try his luck over here," the voice in my head whispered. Then it continued, "He seems to prefer to make his advances on you while you are sleeping and unsuspecting."

I exaggerated a yawn and stretch as I opened my eyes and rubbed at them with my fists. "Morning, Dad."

"Why is this goddamned mutt on your sister's bed?"

Faking the most realistic looking frown that I could, I replied, "Hmm, I didn't realize he had gotten up there. I'm sorry." I knew he wouldn't mention Caroline still being in her day clothes. He wouldn't want me to know his real reason for coming in here in the first place. Then he came towards me with that look in his eyes. They were so bright that they almost looked like they were glowing. I felt my breath catch in my throat and that sick feeling of dread came over me.

Dad's eyes did that. They were blue and they actually changed brightness depending on his mood and the weather. Everyone told me that my eyes did the same thing. My older brother's eyes did it too, so it wasn't that hard for me to believe. My mom had blue eyes as well, but they were darker and stayed that way no matter what. My younger brother and sister seemed to have her blue eyes. But right now my father's eyes were bright with his craziness and that was paralyzing to me.

And, in what couldn't have been a more perfect moment, "Emily?" Caroline's eyes opened and I swear I could actually see them come to focus on our father, "Oh, Daddy. Sorry, I didn't know you were in here." This could turn out one of two ways: he would just make up an excuse for having coming in here to begin with, or he would get violent.

I just wanted him to hurry up and get out of our room. I didn't like being a part of the center of his attention. "Just try to play along with him and maybe you can save the both of you for now," the voice in my head ordered.

I hoped the voice was right, so I played along by saying, "Dad was just in to wake us up. We have a lot of work to do today."

Dad seemed to approve of this with a nod of his head. "She's right. The animals won't feed themselves and we have some planting to do. Now get dressed and come downstairs quick before I take the strap to you both."

"Yes, Dad. We'll be right down."

I wondered what it would be like to look forward to the start of a new day. Never once did I remember having had that feeling. I always dreaded waking up in the morning, or even worse being woken up in the night, in the same house, with nothing new to look forward to and the same worries always being there day after day.

I wouldn't be a child forever. Thank God. Then I would leave this place and my parents and the nightmare would finally be over. It seemed like forever until that day would come. But I had to keep reminding myself that one day it would all be over or I would never make it until then.

"Was that really why Daddy was in here?"

"Yes, shh. Now get dressed. We have to hurry up and get downstairs. He's already in a bad mood." I laid my nightgown over the end of my bed, getting it ready to put on later tonight. I was already dressed in my pants and blue sweatshirt, both hand-me-downs from my older brother Johnny. I whispered to Julie that I would be back later and for her to be a good girl. I was ready to begin the day.

"Hurry up! Do you want to give him a reason to take the belt to you already?" She was taking so long and I was starting to get nervous.

"Okay, I'm ready now, Emily. I'm sorry I can't be as fast as you. These pants are getting too tight." They were actually my old corduroy jeans. Except now they had a hole in the right knee. I would have to remember to look through some of my clothes again and give the smallest ones to her.

Too bad we couldn't just go out and buy some. Sometimes Mom made us new clothes when she got cloth, which was always nice. It had been quite a while since she had made me any clothes though. Neither of our parents worked at an actual job. Not a lot of moms went out to work, but I had read in the newspaper and in the magazines that Mom got about some who did. It was probably best that she was home all day. Otherwise we would be left with our father alone. I didn't care for that idea at all.

I didn't care for that idea either. Things would probably be very different around here if their mother wasn't around most of the day. Their father would have free reign to do as he pleased whenever he pleased. I'm sure their mother being around didn't change very much where that was concerned, but it didn't hurt. Maybe the kids would have gotten tired of the things their father did by now if that were the case and maybe Emily would have allowed me more control by now too. That would be a good thing. Things would be so different. The better thing would be if their father went to work at a real job or left altogether.

CHAPTER FOUR

We lived just outside the small town of Dereves and had a small farm. It was big enough to keep our family fed and we still had plenty to be able to sell for some money at our little produce stand out by the road. We normally had crops of sweet corn, squash, potatoes, radishes, lettuce, onions, carrots, tomatoes, and green peppers. We also had a couple of apple trees, a grape vine, and strawberries.

We kept some animals too. That's why I didn't understand why he had to butcher Whisper. We had a couple of pigs, lots of chickens, a couple of cows (always at least one for milk and at least one to butcher) and even a work horse besides Whisper. A creek ran around two sides of our land, so we even got some fish out of there when we were lucky and anytime we wanted we could catch lots of crayfish. They were pretty good. I thought that life could actually be wonderful if we only had a different father. I was sure too that Mom wouldn't drink like she did if her life was happier and we had a different dad. But we didn't.

I wished that my brothers, my sister and I had a better childhood. I wished that we could go to school like all the other children and make friends. Friends would be great, even to have one friend would be wonderful. Me and my friend could share secrets, wishes, hopes, and dreams. We could play together. Maybe we could even have a secret hide out where we could meet up and spend the night with each other if we wanted. There were so many possible things to be done with a friend. I promised myself that one day I would have a real, true friend that wasn't a doll or related to me.

Johnny and Eric were just about finished with their breakfast already when Caroline and I finally made it to the kitchen. "Girls are so slow," Eric said through a mouthful of egg.

I was already grumpy and answered his rudeness with, "Eew. Don't talk when you're chewing. You're lucky Dad's not right here or he'd backhand you one."

"If you two don't hurry up and eat he's gonna tan both your hides good. He's already working out there. Come on Eric, let's get out there before he gets mad at us," our older brother Johnny's voice of reason broke in. The screen door slammed shut behind them and Caroline and I sat down to our plates.

Was Mom out there helping too? I hadn't seen her when I came downstairs at all. She normally didn't help much with the outside chores. That was normally the boys and Dad. Then I remembered the commotion I had heard last night. She was probably trying to keep clear of us to hide a new bruise or something. I didn't know why she bothered. We all knew what he was like and it was nothing we hadn't already seen before many times. I decided that she must have gone off to hide somewhere after she had made breakfast.

I finished my eggs, toast, and bacon right about the same time as Caroline finished hers. None of it was very yummy after sitting and getting cold for any amount of time, but at least it filled our stomachs up. I took her plate along with mine and sent her outside to start helping Dad and the boys so she wouldn't get into trouble while I did up the morning dishes.

While I washed I worried, as was usual when I was alone, that Dad would come to pay me a visit. But I wasn't allowed to leave dirty dishes in the sink after a meal either. Hopefully he would be too busy with the day's chores to bother me.

I had just finished drying the last dish to be put away when he came to the door. I heard the creak as it opened and then the bang as it slammed shut behind him. Did I jump? I wasn't sure. I didn't look in his direction. Maybe because I was afraid I would scream and run. "You took an awful long time on those dishes Emily." He was coming towards me.

"Just turn around now and run," Julie's voice in my head urged. I wished I had the nerve to just turn and run as she wanted me to.

Instead I said, "I'm sorry. I'm all done now. I'll go right out and get to work." I tried to hurry for the door, knowing it wouldn't be that simple. He grabbed my arm firmly with his big, rough hand that was damp with sweat and led me up to my room. I didn't dare protest. I didn't want my mom or anyone to hear and I didn't want to make him angry.

When he was finished with me I guess he could tell that I was shaken as usual. He told me to go take a quick bath before I came outside to help. I knew why. He wouldn't want anyone to be able to tell by looking at me what he had just done.

My legs felt all shaky and rubbery and my hair was stuck to my face with tears of pain and rage and sweat. My eyes were stinging. My girl parts felt swollen, bruised and torn. The water would help my physical issues somewhat but it could not wash away the way that I felt inside.

I glanced at Julie, who seemed to have an evil plan of some sort. For a moment I swear I saw a vengeful smirk on her face. I assured her that I was okay, put my pants and underwear back on, and obediently went downstairs to the bathroom to take my bath.

I glanced at myself in the mirror as I was taking my clothes off. For a moment I swear I saw someone else in that mirror, someone with brown eyes. I shook my head and looked again, realizing that I was probably just all sorts of screwed up right now because of what Dad had just done to me.

I was a little afraid of what I might see in the mirror, that maybe I had really seen someone else but I had to look. If I didn't look I knew that I would be terrified through my whole bath, imagining stuff that I was worried would come after me or kill me while I washed. I knew the chance that I had just imagined seeing someone else in the mirror was a lot bigger and more likely than the chance that there really was someone else looking back at me.

Quickly I looked back at my image in the mirror so that I wouldn't freak myself out any more than I had already. It was just me looking back with my own blue eyes. Sometimes I was so stupid. With that little problem cleared up, I continued on with getting my bath as fast as I could. I really did not want to end up getting a beating from Dad for taking so long getting outside on top of what had already happened today.

I knew the soap would sting like crazy on my private parts. It always did after my dad did that stuff to me. The sting of my emotions was always worse though. And I needed to clean his grossness from me whether it hurt or not. And get that nasty smell off from me and out of my nose. I didn't think I would ever be able to forget that smell. The smell of his sweat, his nasty, unbrushed, old food and tobacco slobber, and the smell of that gross, disgusting slime. It smelled kind of like old, rotten fish but not exactly. Getting rid of that smell and washing my face and hair was the best part of the bath. It helped me to feel at least a little refreshed, like I was scrubbing my mind as clean as I could of all the dirtiness that had just taken place.

I hurried with the rest of the bath, dried off, and got dressed again. Then I headed towards the kitchen door to go outside, feeling ashamed. My brothers and sister would most likely know what had taken place and look at me all weird. I hated those looks. It didn't matter how I felt though, I had to go help or I would be in huge trouble. What had just happened a little while ago wasn't from being in trouble. That was just because there was something wrong in my father's head. I was sure of that much at least.

Now my mother was in the kitchen. She was wearing her blue

pleated skirt and flowered shirt that I always thought were so beautiful. She had made them herself and I had watched her so she could try to teach me to sew. It looked like she was starting to prepare our supper, with her newly bruised and swollen right cheek. She already had her bottle of whiskey hiding in her apron too. She thought it was hidden, but I could still tell that it was there because of the obvious whiskey bottle shaped bulge.

She scolded me on my way through, sounding more worried than angry, "You should have been out there helping already! That was pretty stupid of you to take your bath before getting all dirty outside anyway. I swear, for being so smart, sometimes you don't think at all! Hurry up and get out there before your father takes your laziness out on everyone else!" She snapped the bean that was in her fingers harder than necessary as if to emphasize what she had said.

In my head I heard Julie say, "Shut up, you stupid drunk. You could change all this, but you don't."

All I could manage to reply to my mother on my way out the screen door was, "Yes, Mom. I'm sorry."

It was too bright outside. I felt used and broken and the rest of the world seemed to have carried on anyways. I was angry that the day was so beautiful. It felt more like it should be a stormy, cloudy, rain pouring from the heavens kind of day to me. But, at the same time, I was also glad the weather was decent for working outside. Dad probably would have made us do the work no matter what the weather was like. I preferred working with the sunshine over pouring rain.

No one looked at me when I joined them outside in the field. I felt ashamed even though I knew the things that happened weren't really my own fault and I think everyone else must have felt just as rotten for me as I felt. At least they didn't look at me in that odd way that meant that they felt sorry for me. I hated that. Dad was at least nice enough to give me some direction by saying, "Emily, you can start by turning some of the soil over there. Make sure you take the rocks out."

"Yes Dad."

We all worked really hard until the sun started to set and it began getting really chilly out. We had one break for lunch in the middle of the day when Mom had brought egg salad sandwiches and ice cold lemonade out to us. We barely talked as we ate and drank while sitting on some newly grown grass next to the corn field we had been seeding. Everyone else must have been as hungry and thirsty as I was. Eric did tell a funny story about the chickens chasing him when he fed them this morning. That had made us all laugh while we ate. Johnny had actually almost choked on a bite that he hadn't swallowed yet because he had laughed so hard.

That break hadn't lasted nearly long enough. I was sore and exhausted and I'm sure my brothers and sister were too. My hands were raw and blistered. My whole body ached all over.

I didn't think that this day would ever end. We all knew better than to complain. I assumed that only because none of us did complain and I know that at least I had wanted to. Finally Mom called out to us that supper was ready. We all paused what we were doing at the same time and looked hopefully at each other and then at my father.

He wiped the sweat from his brow with the sleeve of his plaid shirt. His face was streaked with dirt. Then he nodded and told us, "Go. You kids earned it today." It felt good to hear Dad say that we had actually earned something for a change. We really did work very hard. We probably would have ran to the house if any of us had enough energy left.

Dinner went smoothly. I washed up in the warm water that felt so good even though it stung the new scratches on my sore hands, then sat down and ate quietly alongside my brothers and sister as we were supposed to. Our parents always told us, "no talking at the dinner table," "don't speak unless spoken to," and, "children are to be seen and not heard." I didn't really agree with the rules, but I had no problem at all following them. My experience had always been:

the less attention you received from the Fleischer parents, the better.

None of us chewed with our mouths open. None of us put our elbows on the table. None of us tried to leave the table before everyone else was finished with their suppers. None of us did anything that would upset my father. As I was taking my last bite, (I was normally always the last to be finished eating) Dad spoke.

"Tomorrow I have to go into town to get some more supplies. You boys can do some fishing down at the creek. Try to catch us something good for Sunday's dinner. You girls can help your mom if she needs it. That is, after each of you finish your morning chores, of course."

Johnny and I both said, "Yes, Dad. Thank you."

Caroline and Eric chimed in with, "Yes, thank you, Daddy!"

Then he surprised me by adding, "Emily, tonight I want you to have Caroline help with the dishes. You can have her rinse and dry while you wash. Then you can put them away. She's old enough now to start learning. Got that, Caroline?"

I noticed that my mother gave him a questioning look. Then she must have realized what she was doing and thought about her swollen, bruised face, because she looked back down at her plate instead. It was fine with me if Caroline rinsed and dried the dishes. It would make the work go a lot faster. Caroline seemed excited to be able to help me too and she responded with, "okay, Daddy."

I had made my mind up a few years ago when I was about Caroline's age to stop calling my father Daddy. To me, a daddy was supposed to be like the men in the books that I read: strong and firm, but kind and compassionate. Sometimes giving a spanking, but never beating. Never having the kinds of visits alone with his kids that our father had with us. Daddies were supposed to act like they loved the mommies. I didn't really want to call him Dad either, but I couldn't get away with anything other than that. At least to me calling him Dad felt like I was getting back at him in my own way, even if it was only just a little bit.

"May we start doing the dishes now," I asked.

"Yes, go ahead." So Caroline and I got up from our seats and began clearing the table of the empty dishes. I washed. There were definitely little cuts on my hands from working outside because there were spots that really stung now in the soapy water. Caroline rinsed and then dried. Then I put the clean dishes away while she headed upstairs to our room. The boys had asked while we were still washing and rinsing to be excused from the table.

I wasn't too worried while doing the dishes tonight. The bad thing had already happened this morning. Besides that, I was pretty sure Dad was exhausted from today's work too. Mom was still sitting at the table with him. She seemed like she wanted to say something to my father but was probably waiting until all of us kids were gone from the room to do it. He seemed to be in a pretty decent mood, so she probably figured this was the best time to bring up something important with him. That was what I would probably do if I were her. Being in a good mood wasn't usually like my father, but it was sort of nice for a change.

I finished putting away the dishes in only a couple of minutes. My parents were still sitting at their seats, Dad at the end and Mom in the seat just to his left on the corner. I told them good night and headed up the stairs that led to my room like my brothers and sister had already done.

Caroline was already in her nightgown when I entered our room. I got mine from the end of my bed and put it on as well. "Tomorrow should be a pretty good day," I said to her. She smiled with her awkwardly big teeth that I had learned were common at her age. I was actually a little excited too, maybe even more than a little. I got into my bed and covered up. I turned out the light, gathered Julie in my arms, and said good night to my sister, falling asleep quickly without any problem at all.

I know she's in for a big letdown somehow. There has never

been a good day around this house that didn't come with a hefty price to be paid. Oh well, I guess the sooner she came to terms with the reality of her life and the situation she and her family were in, the sooner she would let me have the control I needed to take care of it all. I knew I could at least save Emily from the pain and anguish, if no one else. Emily was all that really mattered to me anyhow.

CHAPTER FIVE

I was up, dressed, and eating my breakfast earlier than normal that next morning. I even helped Mom cook it. We had buckwheat pancakes with sweet, rich maple syrup that we had made ourselves last year from the sap of our maples. Plus we put juicy strawberries that we had frozen while they were still fresh and ripe from last summer on top. Yummy! I ate three whole pancakes myself.

Mom told me that I just had to help her prepare supper and do the breakfast dishes. She said that I could do as I pleased after that stuff was finished. The boys were out the door to go fishing right after they scarfed their breakfasts down. I'm not sure if they even chewed any of it. I'm sure they were just as excited to go fishing as Caroline and I both were to do whatever we wanted. They were told to go fishing, but I knew they both enjoyed that chore.

I already knew what I wanted to do. I planned on getting a lot of reading and maybe some of my own writing done, under the willow. I loved that tree. I'm not sure why, but I did. Maybe I liked it so much because it looked a little sad to me in a way, which reminded me a lot of myself. I really hoped that Dad would be gone all day long. That would make this the best day I could remember in a very long time.

I helped Mom get supper started before doing the dishes. We were making a pork roast. All I had to do was wash and cut up the potatoes, wash the carrots and cut those up, and the same with the celery. Mom did the onions because she knew they would make my eyes tear up horribly. Then I got the dishes done as quickly as I could.

"Are you sure you don't need me to do anything else, Mom?"

"No. I've got it from here. Go enjoy your day. There probably won't be another like it again for a while." I knew she was right. I think she was almost just as happy for the break from Dad as we were. So I went back to my room and grabbed my doll Julie, my book, my pencil, and my paper.

I walked to my favorite spot on our property: our willow tree that stood halfway between the house and the creek. The branches were so full already and so long that you could pretty much hide from everyone under there. It was like a big umbrella shielding me from everything. I got myself comfortable, sat Julie up against the trunk of the willow, and decided to do a little writing first.

I wrote happy fantasy stories. I couldn't really write anything else, especially not a diary. I wanted to keep a diary, but knew that I couldn't. Someone would surely read it and that would be the end of that and maybe even the end of me too. I wrote a story about a homeless kid and her dog and their adventures together. I dreamed that maybe someday I would be a rich, published author like the people that wrote the books that I had read. That would be something.

After a while I heard my brothers' voices. I looked through the branches and could see them talking excitedly to each other as they walked up from the creek. They had big smiles on their faces, so I stood up and ran over to them. I peeked into the old paint bucket that they were carrying, seeing it was full of fish. "Wow! They were really biting today, weren't they," I said. I was really happy for them.

Eric was the one to pipe up and answer, "Yep! I caught three of them all by myself!" That really was something pretty special. I suddenly felt like playing, instead of sitting still, for a little while.

"Do you guys want to play a quick game of Tag before cleaning the fish? I've been sitting too long," I added.

Johnny declined by saying, "I'll go get started cleaning the fish up. You guys can go ahead and play. Have fun but make sure you don't leave me to do all the work, Eric."

"Nah, I won't. We'll just play a fast game. Promise."

I watched as Johnny headed for the house with the bucket. Then I called out to Caroline to come join me and Eric. She was outside playing with her dolls somewhere, probably near the house. After only a minute or so she came running from the side of the house, just like I had guessed. Before we had a chance to start playing though, Eric surprised me by asking, "First can you read us one of the stories that you made up, Emily?"

"Sure. I guess so." It felt wonderful for Eric to be asking to hear one of my made-up stories. He normally didn't have the patience to sit and listen to a whole story. Maybe this time would be different. I decided to read them the story I had just written. It was a little shorter than my normal stories. "I'll read you guys this one that I just wrote. I think you'll both like it." I was right; they both seemed to love it and sat quietly through the whole thing.

"I'll be 'it' first," I volunteered. I purposely didn't catch Eric and had let him catch me a few times when it was his turn to be "it" after Caroline tagged him. He never seemed to win any of the games that we played, but I was feeling generous because of the great day that we all seemed to be having. We played our game of Tag for probably about half an hour. Then afterwards we each went our separate ways to continue enjoying the rest of our peaceful alone-time. Eric went to help Johnny like he had promised and Caroline took off in the direction she had come from before our little get together.

I felt a little sleepy after our game of Tag and let myself fall asleep for a little bit under the willow with Julie. When I woke up I decided to pull out my book, "Little Women" to read for a while. It was such a good book and I really enjoyed having this time to myself. It was still bright out and my Dad hadn't pulled back into the driveway yet. He was still gone on his errands.

After reading only three pages, I stopped. My tummy was really starting to hurt and I didn't feel so well. I'd have to put the book aside and make a trip in to the bathroom.

I managed to make it into the bathroom and sat down on the toilet. I had diarrhea, again. It had to be my nerves constantly doing this to my body. When I was done and wiped, however, there was blood. From the front. Dad hadn't bothered me at all today though. I suddenly felt scared and really weak.

I would have to tell Mom, but would she be angry with me? And even worse, would she tell Dad? I would have to find out I guess, because I really needed to tell her. The blood wouldn't stop. It just kept dripping and dripping like our leaky bathtub faucet.

I couldn't stop the tears from flowing as I found my mother, sitting at the table, busy folding clothes. She looked up from the towel she was folding and then set it on the table. "What's the matter, Emily?" She sounded genuinely concerned.

"Mom, I don't know what's going on. Something's wrong with my private parts. There's blood and it's not stopping." She laughed. I couldn't believe it! Here I stood crying my eyes out and bleeding from... well, she had no reason to be laughing at me at a time like this.

She got up from her seat and came over to me. She placed her arm around me as she said, "Emily, it's going to be alright. Come with me to the bathroom. I need to have The Talk with you. I should have done it when I noticed you starting to get your boobs." Oh God, what was this all about? Suddenly I no longer felt right with her arm around my shoulders. I let her walk ahead of me to the bathroom as I tried to hide my chest with my arms. Was I going to be punished? Once we were in the bathroom she moved the curtain from under the sink. She brought out the basket with the scrap pieces of cloth in it.

"You have your period. This will happen every month for about a week each time. It's God's way of telling you that you're growing up and it's a good thing to get, because if you don't... that means you've got a baby inside you. But that shouldn't happen until after you're married. Otherwise your father will probably kill you and whatever boy put that baby there. And I would be very disappointed in you. I would not want you to end up like I did." She showed me how to put the cloth into my panties and told me after it was used up how to clean it out.

My head was spinning with thoughts and worries. I was sick to my stomach. This was horrible, not to mention disgusting. I had questions about this that I couldn't ask my mother. What would happen now? I needed to really think about this. But I couldn't do it here or now. It would have to be when I was alone again.

I wasn't in the mood to do anything else. I told my mother that I didn't feel well and was going to go lie down in my bed. She didn't try to argue with me. First I went out and gathered my things from under the willow and brought them with me to my room. I couldn't let those get lost or ruined.

I laid in my bed worrying and thinking. From what my mother had explained to me, it sounded as if I could end up pregnant with a baby because of this bleeding. I was guessing the bad things that my dad did to me were the way a baby got inside someone's belly. That made sense to me. Would I end up pregnant with my father's baby? And if I did, then what would happen? "Everyone would probably blame you and hate you. That's what would happen," said the Julie voice from inside my head. The voice was right, as usual. This was truly awful. Or would he leave me alone now? He must have known for a while how these things worked and I didn't think he would want me to end up with his baby inside me. Ugh. I really didn't feel well at all.

It wasn't too long before Mom called out that dinner was ready. When I stood up from my bed the whole room seemed to spin around me. I just stood there for a minute until things stood still again before heading downstairs.

Dad wasn't home yet. That was nice for a change, although a little weird. We all still ate pretty quietly. I did because I just didn't feel well, and I was still worried. I always seemed to be worrying. The other kids were probably thinking that Mom might tell Dad anything that they did wrong. Which was most likely true. Eric did ask once when Dad would be home. My mother simply said, "When he's done running his errands."

After I finished eating my dinner, Caroline and I washed the dishes together. Our father still wasn't home. I had never known him to be gone so long. I allowed myself to hope just a little that maybe he would never return. We could survive without him, happily too.

Mom was almost passed out at the dinner table. I knew better than to point that out to her. However, I did make sure that I got her attention when I said good night. Once I had woken her up by gently tapping on her when she was passed out like that. That time she had beaten on me herself with the first thing that she could grab, which happened to be her shoe. I had learned my lesson pretty quickly, luckily only suffering a headache because of it.

We would have all gotten into trouble if I didn't try to wake her at all though. We all knew that Dad didn't like it when she passed out like that. He had a hard time waking her to get her to go to bed. They always ended up fighting then too.

Mom lifted her head and opened her eyes a little. "Uh huh," was her only reply as she absently wiped at the drool that was starting to make its way from her mouth down to her chin. I got so frustrated when she was like this. Why did she have to drink so much every day?

I thought the stuff was disgusting myself. I had tasted it once when Johnny had dared me to. Of course I couldn't lose a dare and my parents had both been busy outside doing something at the time. I had taken too big of a sip and almost choked on the nasty stuff. It had made me feel dizzy too, almost right away. Johnny told me I made that part up in my head, but I swear it was true. Drinking that had to be like drinking gasoline or some other poisonous liquid of that sort. I told myself I would never touch the stuff again, dare or no dare.

If she was so miserable in her life she should have just figured out some way to change it. Sure, I know she probably felt trapped and it wouldn't be easy to do. But there had to be some way and she was a grown up. Of course she could find a way if she really wanted to. We would all be much happier. Unless she just left and left us alone with Dad. That would not be good at all. Would she do something like that? Maybe. I wasn't sure. What would I do in her situation? What a big question that was, it was like asking myself exactly what the rest of my life would be like. I had no clue.

For now I just needed to wake her up. I decided to keep the conversation going. Long enough to make sure she stood up and didn't pass back out as soon as I left the room. "The dishes are done and put away, Mom."

"Okay," she said with her slurred speech. I could see her eyes working to open again.

"There was some leftovers that I put away too," now she was beginning to stand up using the table for support. "I made Dad a plate and put it in the refrigerator."

She was finally on her feet. Her eyes were still only half-opened, but she responded again with, "Good." Now she was stumbling off towards the room she shared with our father. I went upstairs to the room I shared with my sister.

What would I do if I were in my mother's position? I didn't think I would ever have to worry about that because I didn't think I would be stupid enough to end up with someone like Dad. But still, it was something interesting to keep in mind. I wouldn't have stayed, that was for sure. I think I would have taken whatever kids I had and left as soon as there were any signs of him being anything like my father was. I wondered if he had always been this way or when the change had started.

I woke the next day to find that Dad had never come home the night before. My hopes that he would never return began to rise to the surface again. I could tell that Mom was worried and irritated that he wasn't home yet because she didn't do any instruction herself that day before our lessons. She just told us to work on our school work ourselves after our morning chores were done. She didn't bother to make breakfast either, just told us to have some cereal or whatever we felt like having.

I decided to have oatmeal and made my brothers and sister some too. It was really delicious with maple syrup, brown sugar, and milk in it. Whenever I ate oatmeal it made me think of the story of "Goldilocks and the Three Bears" with their porridge. I didn't know why, maybe because I always had to wait until the temperature of the oatmeal was just right before I could eat it.

My father didn't come home at all that day. We went about our chores and our school lessons as normal, except without Mom's help. Mom was moody and stayed to herself most of the day. She even told me to figure out supper. I was happy to do it.

It had been another pretty relaxing day so far besides Mom being so miserable and my bleeding. We even played in the yard again for a little while before dinner. Dad still wasn't home by the time we went to bed and Mom was on the couch watching a show on the television. I hated seeing her that way, but I prayed with all my might that night that Dad stayed away forever.

It must have been hours later when I awoke. I felt achy and gross. I must have fallen asleep while praying that my father stayed gone. I looked around and it was still dark. No one except me, Caroline, and Lucky was in our room. I refused to leave the small comfort that was my room to change the soaked rags between my legs until morning. I would just deal with whatever mess there was then.

As I was trying to get comfortable enough to get back to sleep, I heard horrific shrieks coming from somewhere down the hall. That must be what had awoken me. Oh my God! I realized that the shrieks must have come from one of the boys. I wanted to block out the noise, but instead I found myself listening and trying to figure out exactly who was doing the screaming. It sounded as if my father had managed to make it home after all because I heard him mutter a few words that I couldn't quite make out.

My heart was breaking for my brothers. No matter which one it was, the other must be an unwilling witness to whatever horror was taking place. I was pretty sure it must be my little brother Eric, because the screams were more high-pitched than Johnny's would have been. I wished so badly that someone would end this. That the whole nightmare would just go away. And just like that the screams stopped. I listened for a while longer to make sure. Then somehow I managed to force myself to fall back to sleep, holding on to Julie more tightly than ever, feeling relieved after hearing my father's familiar footsteps leave our hallway and head down the stairs.

I wished that Emily hadn't heard those awful screams. I tried to keep her sleeping, but she had forced herself to wake up. From the sound of those screams, I could tell that something terrible must have happened at the hands of Emily's father. Though I had heard cries and such before from her brothers' room, I had never heard anything quite like that. Luckily Emily was able to get herself back to sleep.

I was also more than a little disappointed about her father having returned home after being gone for two whole days. It had been just long enough for Emily to hope that he might never return only to be let down when she realized that he had. I wondered why he had been gone so long, where he had stayed, and what he had done. Maybe we would all find out tomorrow.

CHAPTER SIX

In the morning I went straight downstairs and into the bathroom to change the nasty, blood soaked rags that I now had to wear. And to clean myself up. I brought my change of clothes with me and planned on taking a quick bath while I was in there. The blood had soaked through the rags, my nightgown, and had even gotten on the sheets on my bed. I would have to change my bedding and wash everything that I had bled all over after I finished cleaning myself up. What a long process. I didn't feel like doing it. But I would have to. So I left Caroline sleeping and got busy doing what needed to be done.

The bath was nice even though the water turned pink with the blood that I washed from myself. That was a little yucky, but at least I had washed my hair before the water got all gross. While dressing I made sure to put a couple of fresh rags in my underwear. It felt bulky and uncomfortable, but at least I wouldn't bleed all over the place.

Now I was all cleaned up and dressed. So I gathered up the blood soaked rags, my nightgown and underwear and headed back to the bedroom for my dirty sheets. I grabbed some clean ones from the hall closet and replaced the ones that I took off of my bed. Caroline was still sleeping soundly. I left her and went downstairs into the cellar to throw my load of wash in.

Once that dirty chore was done, I headed back upstairs and out to the kitchen to get some toast. I wasn't very hungry, but knew I needed to eat something because I felt weak and dizzy. But once there I found my father, mother, and Johnny already sitting at the table. Their heads were downcast. My mind replayed the screams that I had heard in the night. My heart sank into my stomach.

"Where's Eric?" I was afraid to hear the answer. I guess I knew deep down inside that something horrible had happened to my little brother.

"Run now Emily! You don't want to hear this," Julie tried to warn me from inside my head.

"Sit down Emily," my father said solemnly.

"No! No, I will not sit down! What did you do to him, you monster!?"

My mother gasped. "Emily! How dare you speak to your father that way! There was a terrible accident last night. Your brother... he didn't make it. We'll bury him ourselves today in the garden." My teeth were clenched together. I knew that they were lying about an accident. I had heard his horrific last cries in the night. Our father did this.

I looked at Johnny. His face was covered in a ghastly, haunted look. And his eyes actually looked gray. Whatever had happened scared the blue right out of Johnny's eyes. He gently shook his head at me, confirming what I had already known. I ran to my room. I couldn't be near my parents right now. Maybe not ever again.

When I got to the room and shut the door, Caroline asked me what was wrong. I couldn't even breathe long enough to tell her. The answer came in between broken sobs and gasps for air. I simply told her that our little brother was dead. That's all I knew for a fact. There was no point in adding to her grief by telling her my suspicions because of what I had heard in the night. She cried and I held her.

It wasn't that I thought that she would yell at our parents like I had yelled at my father if I told her what I thought. But she might end up asking questions that were better left unanswered. It would be better for all of us probably if they stayed that way.

I wondered if it was normal to bury dead people in one's own garden. I knew there were graveyards for that sort of thing, but maybe not for people like us. We didn't go to a church. Our father taught us what he wanted us to know of The Bible and God. Our mother told us the rest when he wasn't around.

So Fleischer's, at least Fleischer children, didn't deserve a burial in a real graveyard like other people. We were no better than our animals. Not even important enough when we died, or were murdered. Nobody cared about us. Nobody. We really were completely on our own; all alone.

I cried and I prayed. I prayed so hard, convinced that someday my prayers would be answered. I had to believe that. I did believe that with all my heart and mind. God must be a very busy man of course and there were probably people in the world with worse problems than mine. I cried until I was too exhausted to even think anymore. Then I slept.

Johnny woke me sometime later. It was time to bury my little brother and he didn't want me to miss it. Eric deserved at the very least for all of us to be there to say our final goodbyes to him.

At least the weather was appropriate for today's occasion. It was gloomy and there was a cold, drizzling rain. I joined Caroline and Johnny in front of the ground that was already dug up for our brother's body to lie in. I couldn't tell anymore if there were tears streaming down from my eyes or if it was just the rain. They felt like one and the same to me at that point.

My parents came out carrying Eric, covered in our best sheet. We wouldn't see his face. Caroline burst out with a gut-wrenching sob. I held her head in my arms against my chest as they lowered him gently into the earth. I barely noticed as Caroline's tears and snot mixed with the rain on my sweatshirt, soaking through to my already cold skin.

Then our parents told us to each take a handful of dirt near the hole and throw it over Eric's body. That seemed wrong to me, but they insisted that's how it was supposed to be done. So Johnny, Caroline, and I each took a turn throwing wet dirt on the sheet that covered my brother's dead body, followed by each of my parents doing the same thing.

I wanted to speak. All of a sudden I just felt like I had to, for Eric. And for myself, Johnny, and Caroline. With a voice that was hoarse from crying so much I said, "Can I say something about Eric at least? In the books they always say something nice when they bury someone."

"Go ahead Emily," my mother seemed to welcome the interruption.

I did cry throughout my little speech, but at least I would be able to remember that I had done it. I had paid the best respect to Eric that I could. I had read about someone else doing the same thing when they buried their pet. "Eric, you were the best little brother anyone could ever ask for. You annoyed us, you made us laugh and you got us into trouble sometimes. Above everything else you were one of us. I know you're in a better place now. No more chores, no more pain. No more tears. Enjoy yourself and know that we'll all come to play with you again someday. I love you and I will never forget you, Eric Ryan Fleischer."

Johnny patted my shoulder as I walked past him to go back into the house. Caroline followed me in. I didn't know if we were supposed to stay to help fill in the rest of Eric's grave or not. I didn't want to. Dad could punish me if he felt like it. A little bit of pain would be fine with me right now. I was already in so much pain on the inside. Why not match that with pain from the outside?

As I entered the house, a familiar smell pierced my nostrils. Fish baking, making my heart ache again. I had forgotten that we were supposed to eat the fish for dinner tonight that Johnny and Eric caught only the day before yesterday. I swore that I could still hear him saying, "I caught three of them myself!" My stomach rumbled. I knew that I was hungry because I hadn't eaten all day, but I didn't think that I'd be able to eat. Maybe I would be able to stomach a little something. I decided I would at least try.

I went straight to my room to change out of my clothes that were wet from the rain. I had a headache. My eyes felt like they had been lit on fire. My throat felt like someone had tied it in a knot. And my stomach. Ugh. My stomach was twisting and turning like it always did before I threw up or had diarrhea. But this time I was sure there was nothing in it to puke or poop.

It was hard to believe that only yesterday Eric was here with us and we had had such a good day. And the day before that had been even better. Mom and I had made a delicious breakfast together, Johnny and Eric had gone fishing and caught lots of fish, I had read Caroline and Eric a story and then the three of us had played Tag, and Dad had stayed gone for two whole days, until all of the rest of us were in bed last night. I would gladly give it back if only Eric could be here with us again.

At dinner Dad did make mention of the fact that we were eating the very last meal that Eric would be able to help put on the table. We kids all seemed to only nibble at our food. I hadn't eaten anything else all day, but it seemed so hard to swallow with the knot that was in my throat. Dad ate as if he hadn't eaten in forever and Mom just ate like she normally would on any ordinary day. Ugh. They made me sick just watching them go on like nothing had changed.

Eric's seat at the table next to Mom was empty. Empty for God's sake! Didn't they realize that? His place at the table, his bed, his clothes, everything of his would be empty now. Without him. Johnny didn't play with us very much anymore so now Caroline and I wouldn't be able to play the games we usually played. No more Hide and Seek, no more Tag. You couldn't really play those games very well with only two people. Things were going to be different. That much was for certain.

After dinner I washed the dishes with Caroline's help. Then I went outside to the spot where Eric was buried. There was a medium sized stone laying there. Chiseled into it was this:

Eric Ryan Fleischer
1969-1976

That was nice. It didn't seem like enough, but it would have to do. "Hey, I'm surprised there's even that here. Think about it: your Dad wouldn't want anyone outside the family knowing about how Eric died or where his final resting spot is," said the Julie in my head.

Of course, she was right. Again. I sighed and said, "goodnight," to the grave where Eric now rested and walked back into the house.

I couldn't stop thinking about Eric. About my little sweet brother spending the night alone out beneath the dirt. About how he had actually spent his last moments alive. That part I didn't know for sure and I didn't really want to, but my imagination just would not leave the matter alone. I wondered if I would have to add nightmares about poor Eric to the list of things that disturbed my sleep. Probably.

Here I was again, laying in my bed, thinking. I could run away. But I knew I couldn't do that to my remaining brother and my sister. And where would I go? I'd probably be caught anyway and the punishment I would receive was unthinkable, even to me. Maybe the three of us could run away together. Of course, then we would probably all get caught and be in terrible trouble. And I would end up feeling bad because it would have been my idea.

This torment of my family had to end. Somehow, I had to figure out a way. Maybe I could tell someone what was going on. "Are you crazy? I cannot believe you just thought that. Who would you even tell that would believe you? What would happen after you told the story of the nightmare you guys are living? Would it make things better or even worse?" Julie was right. She always seemed to be right. In the end, I thought it better not to tell. The possible consequences were far too horrible to even imagine.

I asked Johnny once about the strange voice in my head, the Julie voice. He acted as if it were a silly question from a funny little kid. I had been completely serious when I asked though. I had been really concerned that I wasn't right in the head. He had attempted to reassure me that I was completely normal by saying, "Emily, everyone has a little voice in their head that talks to them and tells them what they should and shouldn't do. It's called your conscience. Pinocchio's conscience was Jiminy Cricket. Remember that story?" I did. That made sense to me and made me feel better.

I can assure you that I am not just some unimportant little voice in Emily's head. I am not just her conscience. I know what a conscience is and I have my own. I'm a separate person. I'm part of Emily, but I'm very different. Telling someone what her father is doing would be a huge mistake. I just know it. There has to be a different way to take care of the problem, her father, and to take care of it for good. He killed her little brother already, who would be next? I now realized that there was nothing that he was not capable of doing.

CHAPTER SEVEN

I heard my mother holler at my father. It sounded like they were in their bedroom. Their voices were muffled as if they were behind a closed door. But I could still hear them and knew that this was going to be bad. Mom never yelled at Dad. Ever. I wondered if he would kill her like he had killed my little brother. Would he end up killing us all in the end?

What was she hollering at him about anyway? Was it about Eric? I couldn't hear well enough, no matter how hard I tried. I did hear someone or something smashing into the furniture or the walls, or maybe both. That was followed by more screaming and shouting. The screaming came from my mother and the shouting was all from my father now.

Then a strange idea came to me for some reason. If I cut my tongue off, I wouldn't be able to tell. It would no longer be my fault that I couldn't save us. People would understand that I wasn't to blame if I had no tongue to speak with. Before I had a chance to think the idea through, I proceeded to sneak out of my room and down the dark hallway to get the shears. It just felt like I had to do it.

I had to hurry before anyone caught me out of bed. In the bathroom, I began carrying out my ill thought of plan. I stuck my tongue out as far as I could and opened the scissors, sticking my tongue between the blades. And then I closed the shears, waiting for the pain my sliced tongue would create. I was a little relieved but also disappointed when my tongue only slid out from between the blades. I tried again but the same thing happened. I couldn't cut my own tongue off. It was too slippery or these scissors were too dull. They were also dirty, tasting like metal and blood or something disgusting.

Without accomplishing what I had come all the way down here in the dark of the night by myself to do, I quietly brought the shears back to where they belonged. Then I headed back to my bedroom. What a stupid idea that was anyway! What was I thinking? I wasn't. Could that have been one of Julie's ideas maybe? This time I didn't think so. I was just desperate for the nightmare to end, and I could hear that my parents were still fighting. This was the longest fight I could ever remember between them.

I considered killing myself. But I had always been taught that if you killed yourself you wouldn't go to Heaven. You would go to Hell instead. And I felt like I was already in Hell. I didn't want to live anything like this for all of eternity. I was also taught that it was a chicken's way out. Besides that, I still held on to the dream that one day I would be rescued from this life by a wonderful man and we would get married, have children, and live happily ever after. I had read about it. Why couldn't it happen for me too?

"It's not going to happen like that for you and you know it. It probably doesn't happen in real life for anyone except for in those stupid books. Marriage is for idiots and men are no good. You need to stop fantasizing about this stupid fairytale you keep thinking is going to happen and wake up to reality," Julie said in my head.

If I wanted this to end I guess my only option would be to tell my mother. She would have to figure out a way to bring an end to this. She wouldn't let it go on. "Are you stupid?! She isn't going to do a damn thing and you know it," Julie criticized. It was a scary idea, my tummy got all bubbly just thinking about it, but then this would finally end. It had to end and this was the best solution I could come up with. It was hard to get to sleep my heart was beating so funny, but eventually I did, holding Julie tightly so she wouldn't take off and cause trouble or do anything bad to me.

A week or so went by. Maybe it had been two weeks. We woke each morning, ate our breakfasts, did our morning chores, did our school work, and then did the rest of our chores before dinner and bed. There was a time or two when I probably could have told Mom the horrible secret that I was keeping, but each time I thought of a reason why it wasn't the right time. When I went to bed that night, I decided that tomorrow would be the day I told my mother, no matter what.

I woke up that next morning because of a scary dream. All I could remember from it was that Eric had climbed out of his grave in the garden and tried to go upstairs to his own bed, tracking dirt all through the house as he did. Julie had stopped him somehow and made him go back to his cold, lonely resting place. More heartache, more fear. I wiped that from my mind as best as I could for now. I had something important to do that should have been done long ago, whether Julie thought so or not.

My tummy was all twisty and bubbly again, or still, I didn't even know which anymore. At least the bleeding had stopped several days ago. For this month I guess. Mom was alone and not yet drunk. Now was my chance to tell her. I went into the kitchen. "Mom?"

"Yes, Emily?"

"I need to tell you something."

"Yes?"

She was staring straight at me. My heart started beating really fast and hard again. I could feel the beating in my chest, arms, neck and face.

It was hard to look at her. Her nose was crooked and swollen; both of her eyes were black and blue. Well, more red and black than black and blue. Her right eye looked almost swollen shut. It looked like it must really hurt.

Actually, she looked sore even just sitting there cutting up the carrots. It seemed as if it took all of her effort to lift her arm from the table without letting out a scream. She was sitting awkwardly in the chair with a grimace that gave away the pain that she was trying so hard to hide. He must have really hurt her last night during that fight. I felt bad for her and started to reconsider telling her what was on my mind. She had barely finished healing from their last bad fight. But I had to tell her. No matter what the consequences ended up being. "Don't do it Emily! She's not going to listen and you know it," the Julie in my head said.

My face felt like it would melt right off my bones and my stomach wouldn't last much longer before I had to use the bathroom. I thought my heart might actually pop right out of my chest.
"It's about Dad. Um..."

"What Emily? Spit it out already!" She stopped chopping the carrots to focus solely on me and what I was going to tell her.

"Never mind. I forgot." I focused my eyes on her hands and kept them there.

"Emily Ruth, you tell me right now and stop your lying. I can tell you've got something important on your mind. Now say it." I giggled. I couldn't help it. I was so nervous and it just came out. It was either giggle or cry. If I had started crying just then, I don't think that I would have ever been able to stop again.

Okay, just say it Emily. This is it. "Dad does bad things to my privates. He's really mean to all of us kids, even to the boys. Well, not Eric anymore." She started chopping the carrots again. Her lips were pressed together and thinned out. She was angry. Good. She should be. I peed my pants a little on accident. It was warm, wet, and just a little uncomfortable.

"How dare you," she slammed the knife down onto the table and almost howled at the pain it must have caused. "What the Hell is wrong with you?" Could she tell that I had just peed some in my pants? "Just because you don't like the way things are doesn't mean you can make up these kinds of lies about your father."

"But Mom..."

"Don't but-Mom-me you lying bitch! Just wait till he hears about this."

I was crying now. He would kill me for sure, or at least make me wish that he had.

"Mom! No! Please!"

"Get the fuck out of my face." She got up from the table and grabbed her bottle of booze from the cupboard, not even caring that I was still standing there watching. I passed gas that ended up being more than gas, and peed some more. My heart was still beating so hard that it felt like it would burst right out of my chest. After it was done breaking. I had to go to the bathroom and clean myself up. Then I'd have to go to my room to change my pants and underwear. I felt filthy inside and out.

I couldn't believe that my mother didn't believe me. How could she think that I would make something like that up? She knew that I would be severely punished if she told my father what I had told her. How could she do that to me? Why couldn't she have just believed me? Julie answered quietly in my head, "Because she's a selfish bitch and cares more about herself than you or her other kids. She's a scaredy cat, scared of your father as much as you are. You can't count on her." I would never call my mother that and I didn't believe it. I think she cared about us kids more than she cared about herself but she probably was terrified of my Dad. I didn't blame her for that.

A little while later my father came to the door of my room with the ax in his hand and simply said, "Come on."

I still had the snots and tears on my face from telling Mom. I wiped at them with the sleeve of my shirt and dutifully got up off my bed. I followed my father down the stairs and outside. The bright light of the day made me angry and hurt my head. The sun had no business shining. Not today.

I imagined Julie jumping up off the bed and chasing after my father. She jumped on his back and just started biting chunks from his flesh. I almost wished that would really happen. I knew that was all just my crazy imagination though.

What was he going to do to me? Where was he taking me? Was he going to make me chop off one of my own body parts? Whatever he was taking me to do I knew I was going to hate it. He wasn't going to let me get off easily for what I had done. I supposed it would be better to get my punishment done and over with, no matter what it was. If I happened to die, at least I hadn't killed myself and I would still go to Heaven.

At least the house always appeared gloomy. The house must at least know what miserable things took place here and sympathetically cast the right mood. No matter how much we cleaned and scrubbed and dusted, it seemed like there would always be a layer of dirt and dust on everything. Everything was torn and worn. Even the people. God didn't seem to extend the same courtesy with the weather.

My father brought me to the maple tree where Lucky was tied up and handed me the ax. What he expected me to do suddenly sank into my head. Oh God, please no. "This is dinner. Get it butchered and cleaned up quick so it can get cooking. Next time maybe you'll remember to keep your whore mouth shut." I didn't dare say a word. I just stood there until he left for the house.

Lucky whined at me. He was probably wondering why I wasn't paying any attention to him. I couldn't do this. God, help me! Or kill me and get it over with! I can't do this anymore! I sat down on the hard ground that was bumpy with roots next to my dog and hugged him close to me, "I'm so sorry Lucky! I love you. Please, please know that." Salty tears or snot or both made their way into my mouth. Lucky licked some of my tears away. Then I set him back down and stood up with the ax. I wished that my father had brought me out here with the ax to kill me instead.

I closed my eyes and tried to pretend my beloved Lucky was one of the chickens. I had never even had to butcher one of them yet. All I knew was that the boys chopped their heads off and then they ran around as if they were searching for their severed part. Hopefully it would be different with a dog. I didn't think I could bear it if he didn't actually die right away. He yelped once as the very last tear I vowed to shed fell to the dirt. I vomited from a combination of the sight of Lucky laying there bloody with his head almost completely separate from the rest of his body because of me and from grief over what I had just done. He didn't run around and never would again. I would not be eating dinner this evening, beating or not.

I was done caring. I was too emotionally exhausted from years upon years of being mistreated, beaten, and used. My beautiful horse, my baby brother, and now my beloved dog were gone. Who was next? If my father had been trying to break my spirit, he succeeded. However, he also succeeded in making me feel like I had nothing left to lose that wasn't at risk of being lost anyway if I didn't do something to end things. If I had to, I would die trying.

I picked my bloodied pet Lucky up as gently as I could (as if that would make some sort of a difference) and carried his still warm, but lifeless body back to the house. I laid him in the center of the kitchen table just the way he was, in almost two separate, blood soaked pieces. Some of the skin on his neck had stayed attached, so his head wasn't completely severed.

My mother watched me, looking shocked, as I laid our bloody pet on the center of the table and then she asked, "What the hell is this?"

"This is your dinner! Clean it yourself, Mother!"

I stomped down the hall into the bathroom, slammed the door shut behind me, and scrubbed as hard as I could at my hands and arms. I would probably feel Lucky's blood on me for a long time to come. Afterwards, when my hands and arms were red and raw from being scrubbed so hard, I went up to my room still shaking from what I had done. I hoped to be able to stay there for the rest of the evening.

Why didn't Emily let me handle the Lucky situation? She shouldn't have had to do that, not by herself. When will she let me help her? When will she finally see that she won't be able to survive without my help? Hopefully the time will come soon, before it's too late for her. The next question was: what in the world was wrong with that man and what was next? I hated just sitting back and having to watch the things he put Emily through. No one should have to go through the types of things that she did every day.

CHAPTER EIGHT

I was amazed when no one bothered coming to my room at all. My father didn't come to beat me for being disrespectful to my mother or to beat me for not finishing the job of getting dinner fully cleaned. No one came to tell me to come down to dinner and no one come to tell me it was time to do the dishes.

The first person I saw again that evening was Caroline when she came in to get ready for bed. She seemed awfully cheerful as she said, "I did the supper dishes all by myself tonight. Daddy let me. Oops. I forgot. We aren't supposed to talk to you."

Oh, they were supposed to give me the silent treatment as part of my punishment. That was fine with me. "I'm tired. I'm going to sleep. Good night." I covered myself up, snuggled close to my doll, and closed my eyes. Caroline got ready for bed quickly and turned out the light.

I expected my father to come to my room that night. I didn't change out of my pants and shirt on purpose. Julie was the one that had suggested I do that. We both agreed that it probably wouldn't stop him from doing what he wanted, but it would slow him down and make it easier to fight back.

I had tried my hardest not to fall asleep as I listened to every creak, waiting for the sound that would warn me he was on his way. It didn't matter either way, awake or asleep he would make sure he got what he came for. I eventually lost the battle to exhaustion and woke up as I heard our bedroom door open. At least my bleeding had stopped. I shouldn't be embarrassed about that, considering what he was going to do to me, but I couldn't help it. He didn't speak. He never did and tonight was no different. Except that I wasn't just going to lay there and pretend that nothing was happening tonight.

My father wrestled with my pants. Especially to get them down from around my butt and thighs. I wiggled my hips and held onto my pants using my belt loops, trying to keep them from being pulled off. He yanked hard, making my pants dig into my bruised skin on their way down. I think one of my fingers was pulled out of its socket too or sprained at least. My pants had ripped.

He was grunting. He reeked of whiskey and sweat and his hands felt like wet sandpaper on my raw skin. I continued to wriggle around, trying to make him give up for the night. My muscles were getting tired fighting against someone so much bigger and stronger than I was. I knew it was a losing battle, but fighting was all I had left to do.

Then my father flipped me over onto my stomach and just laid his whole body on mine in order to hold me down. I could feel his nasty privates against my naked butt and that slime. It was like the trail a snail leaves behind. Using his arms to hold my top half down, he repositioned himself. Then he spread my legs apart with his own. I couldn't fight in this position. I tried swinging my head back to hit my father's, but his head wasn't close enough to mine.

All of his weight rested on the left side of my chest as he used his right hand to find the spot he was looking for. Where he intended to force his thing to fit. My arms were stuck under me, they were falling asleep and some of my hair was in my mouth. It was hard to breathe with all his weight pressing on me. Maybe I would get lucky and die before he actually started.

My skin down there was too dry for what my father was trying to do. I felt his dry skin grabbing and dragging at mine. Normally he spit down there to make things easier for him, but I must have put up too much of a fight for him to bother with that tonight. He kept pushing anyways. It felt like his thing would drill a new hole that didn't belong. I wished there were no holes at all down there. His pushing was tearing my skin. Then I felt a sharp pain and there was something wet and sticky where it had just been dry.

My skin must have torn. It had done that before. It stung a lot, but hurt a little less with the wetness now. He pushed inside. A little at first, the pain was already unbearable. Then he pushed further and I couldn't help but scream out in pain. Luckily the pillow was right in front of my face, so I used that to help muffle the sound. It felt as if his thing would push right out the front of my stomach. I didn't know why I thought it was so horrible to scream, to try to alert someone else of what was happening, but I did. I think maybe I still felt ashamed at the idea of being found in such a position and I was worried that someone else would have to suffer because of me. I didn't want that.

A couple more of those painful thrusts and then he stopped, filling me with that wet, gross ooze. He was finally done. He climbed off me, pulled his pants back on and then finally left our room.

I was sore, swollen, stinging, and bloody. I knew from previous experience that it would sting really badly again when I went pee in the morning. I would have to remember to pat instead of wipe dry.

Telling my mother hadn't worked. In fact it had only managed to make me more of a target for my father's anger or whatever it was. And now my mother acted like she hated me too. Hopefully, my brother and sister were just doing as they were told by ignoring me so that they wouldn't get into trouble themselves. Maybe they had been told some sort of a lie about what I had done. What would I do? There was no one else that I could tell. Everyone here already knew the things that Dad did, even if some of the ones that knew refused to believe it.

I forced myself to fall asleep holding Julie while thinking of Candy Land. Candy Land was a wonderful world. Everything there was made of candy and chocolate. Even parts of the people were made that way. And everyone there was sweet. Sweet like warmhearted, not sweet like yummy. The water was flowing, bubbly chocolate. The grass was lush, green licorice. The bark of the trees was actually peanut brittle. The sun was constantly shining. It was beautiful there. The first book I published was going to be Candy Land when I left this nightmare of a life behind. People of all ages would read it and love it.

I wouldn't use my last name either. I didn't want to be a Fleischer anymore. I wish I never had been at all. If I had to I would just be Emily Ruth. No Fleischer. Even though Ruth was after my mother. Maybe I would just be Emily. No middle name and no last name. Candy Land by Author Emily. That sounded really good. I started to drift off to sleep.

I hoped that one day Emily's dream of being a writer really came true. In the meantime, she needed to let me help her in order to survive. I could not understand why she hadn't let me in yet. Yes, she let me give her small suggestions here and there, but she never let me have the control that I needed to shield her and really take care of things. There had been a few things that she saw and heard over the years that she somehow managed to block from her memory with my help, but not everything that she should have. I just had to bide my time until she was ready.

CHAPTER NINE

In the morning I went about my business as if the day before had never happened. Caroline was already gone from our room. I got dressed, made my bed, and went downstairs to breakfast. Nobody was in the kitchen. There were dishes dirty with toast crumbs and egg yolk sitting on the counter next to the sink, but no breakfast sitting anywhere for me. I made myself some toast with peanut butter and ate that. It was nice to have something different to eat every once in a while anyways. Then I washed the dishes.

I looked outside for the rest of my family. My mother wasn't out there but my brother, sister, and father were. Caroline and Dad were planting more seeds by the looks of it. Johnny was tending the animals. I figured I'd better get out there to help.

Johnny looked up at me when I came out and then looked quickly away. Caroline appeared as if she were purposely not looking in my direction. My father didn't say anything or look at me at all either. I didn't know what I was supposed to do. I felt so lost and alone. So as much as I didn't want to, I asked, "Dad, what can I do to help?"

"I don't need you. Get back in the house before I whip you for daring to even speak to me." His words stung. Everyone acted as if I was the one who had done something wrong instead of my father.

Instead of saying anything further, I went back in.

I looked around the gloomy house for my mother and found her in the cellar taking clothes from the washer. I hated the cellar. It was dark and smelled musty. There wasn't really a floor to speak of, it was just dirt. Sometimes you could see a rat or two running off to hide somewhere. The stairs leading to the cellar were scary too. They were steep and made of rock or cement, something like that. I didn't trust them. "Do you want me to hang those?"

I was told to, "Go and scrub the bathroom instead. The dirtiest child can do the nastiest chore," that's what she said to me. She may as well have slapped me hard across my face.

I spent a long time cleaning that bathroom. I had nothing better to do and I needed to burn my frustrated energy on something. First I scrubbed the walls, even using a rag on the end of the mop to reach to the top and the ceiling. Then I scrubbed the tub. Then the sink. Next the toilet. Last I scrubbed the floor. By the time I finished I ached all over.

My father came into the house. He announced that he was making a trip to the dump and that he was taking me with him. I really didn't want to go. I tried to act like I still had work to do on the bathroom, but both of my parents could tell that I had finished the basics long beforehand. So I went out and got into the passenger's side of our pickup without any further protests.

It was an uncomfortably quiet ride. I normally didn't mind the quiet. But here, there was hatred in the air. I loathed my father but now I knew for sure that he despised me as well. Why did he want me to go with him so badly all of a sudden? Was it because he thought I was trash now too? "You're not trash. You have to remember that. It's your father and your mother that are the garbage," Julie tried to reassure me in my head.

He slowed the truck and pulled over on the side of the road. We were in the middle of nowhere. The dump was way out in the middle of nowhere too, but we were definitely not at the dump. There were some woods out the window on his side of the road. On my side there just appeared to be never ending hills of green grass.

He undid the buckle of his belt on his pants. "Emily, get out and run! Just go," Julie urged, obviously knowing what was coming next.

He made me put his thing in my mouth. It smelled gross, kind of like fish, and tasted much worse. There was something flaking off his skin as he pushed my head repeatedly to make his thing move in and out. I kept gagging but he yelled at me not to dare stop.

After what seemed like forever, he did that nasty, disgusting thing right in my mouth and I couldn't help it. I threw up out the window on my side. My father was lucky, or maybe I was, that I was able to make it out the window. My mouth was sore and my jaw was tired. The whole thing was awful.

While I was throwing up I heard the sputtering engine of a car. It stopped and I heard a car door shut. Then a very well dressed man who looked to be about my father's age was at our driver's side window. He took off his hat and asked, "Is everything alright here?" I was still gagging and throwing up, so I couldn't say anything. I should have made myself say something. Or I should have at least shaken my head to indicate that everything was indeed not alright.

My father only said, "Oh yes. I appreciate your concern Sir, but everything is fine. I just pulled over because my daughter said that she was going to be sick. You okay now, Honey?"

I didn't even get a chance at all to respond. The man simply said, "Okay, just checking if you needed any help. You folks have a nice day." He tipped his hat as he placed it back on his head. He was back in his car, already pulling away, by the time I pulled myself back together. I was upset with myself for the lost opportunity of possible escape. To try to avoid my father, I focused my attention out the window on my side and noticed that some of my puke was dripping down the side of the truck. Gross.

When the other man's car was completely out of sight my father grabbed me by my hair. He pulled me from the truck and shoved me by my ponytail across the road and over to the woods. He walked me through them, making me trip on twigs and stones, for long enough so that I could no longer see the road, just trees. The trees blotted out the light of the sun. It was cold and smelled of pine. He threw me to the ground by my hair. There were roots of trees sticking up out of the ground, rocks, branches and pine needles. The ground was damp. This seemed eerily similar to my reoccurring nightmare.

I tried to fight him. He punched me hard in the face and then I must have blacked out. When I came to again, I could hear my father's belt buckle jingle as he pulled his pants back up. My pants were lying next to me in a pile on the ground. I hurt. My face, my backside, my private parts, I couldn't think of a place that didn't hurt. I slid my pants back on over my scraped up legs and stood in order to pull them up.

I was dizzy and my right eye wouldn't open. We walked, me more stumbling than walking, back to the truck without exchanging any words. The rest of the trip to the dump was just as quiet and so was the ride back home.

When I walked through the front door of our house my mother looked at my face and frowned. She didn't say anything, just grabbed a piece of beef from the refrigerator and stuck it in my hand. Then she moved my meat laden hand to my sore face. I saw her give my father a quick look of disapproval. That was all. Nobody spoke to me the rest of the day.

Emily had blacked out in the woods, but I was still there. I witnessed everything that horrible man did. He used that poor little girl's body in every way imaginable while she was out of it. I'm glad she wasn't awake and aware while he did those things to her. What a disgusting excuse for a human being he was. Why did he do those things to his own children? I guess the reason didn't really matter. The truth was that there was no reason good enough to excuse the things that he did.

CHAPTER TEN

A couple of days later they, meaning my parents that hated me, made me help them move the stuff that was mine from my bedroom into the cellar. With the dirt floor and the rats, the musty smell and the dark that the lights didn't seem to break through, the cobwebs and the spiders. Caroline got to keep the dresser with the drawers that liked to stick. I would have to use my nightstand for my clothes.

I hated my new room as much as I now hated my life. I had thought it was miserable before, but life had managed to reach a new level of horrible. I supposed I should be grateful that I at least got to keep my clothes, bed, blankets, and Julie. They tried to make it sound like a good thing, like I was getting my very own room because of the fact that I was getting older. I knew that my father just wanted to separate my sister and me. Maybe my mother wanted to separate us as well in order to keep my influence as far away from Caroline as she could.

I would be spending as little time as possible down here. I didn't know how I would ever sleep here in this dungeon. There was no way to even pretty it up. I think the little area that was my new room actually used to be our old root cellar. I guess that was what my parents had called it. It was where we used to store some of our vegetables and fruits during the cold months to make them last until the next season. For the past few years Mom had been canning what she could and putting it in the refrigerator and cutting up and freezing what could be frozen.

I got ready and lay in my bed. I closed my eyes, hugged Julie, and tried to pretend that I was still in my old bedroom upstairs. I tried so hard but that didn't matter. I just couldn't ignore the cellar smell, the cellar dark or the feeling of being completely alone, except for the many rodents that I was sure were down there with me.

I thought again of running away. I could leave while everyone was sleeping and be miles from here before anyone even realized that I was gone. And then what about Johnny and Caroline? I didn't have to run away tonight. In fact, I wasn't ready to run away tonight. A real plan would have to be made and I would offer my siblings the chance to leave with me. My new idea left me feeling hopeful and I was finally able to fall asleep.

I slept fitfully amongst my all too familiar monster under the bed, Eric under the cold ground just on the other side of the cellar wall, Julie plotting something evil that I couldn't stop, and some new dungeon monsters.

I woke up the next day tired and confused about my whereabouts and what time of day it might be. After accidentally rubbing my hand across my still bruised eye, I soon remembered my newest situation.

I searched for the string that hung from the light fixture. I found it and pulled until it clicked and the dim light made my even dimmer situation a little clearer. I got my clothes from my nightstand and got dressed. Then I made my bed and set Julie on the pillow like I did every other morning. I went upstairs not knowing what time of day it was.

My mother was at the stove and I could smell bacon and eggs cooking. The sun was shining brightly through the kitchen windows. I wasn't sure whether I should say good morning or not but I did it anyway, leaving out the word "good" on purpose. "Morning. Do you want any help?"

She didn't look at me, but she did at least respond, "You can set the table for me. Your sister is in the bathroom. She has been helping me cook." A very unsettling feeling came over me. I felt almost as if Caroline were being trained to replace me.

During breakfast Julie tried to help me plot. "You'll need to plan your getaway with Johnny and Caroline and fast. Something bad is going to happen again soon, I just have a feeling." Her words gave me that yucky stomach feeling. I wanted to do as she said, I just had to figure out if I would still go if Johnny and Caroline chose not to go with me but, instead, to stay behind. Would I be able to leave without them, knowing that they were still here? And would they rat me out to Mom and Dad? For that last question I would just have to pray the answer was no.

A few days later, after I had washed and put away the breakfast dishes I finally found an opportunity to speak alone with Johnny. He was outside feeding the chickens. Mom was elsewhere in the house cleaning whatever she had decided was dusty or dirty probably. Dad had left right after breakfast to run some errands with Caroline. I only hoped that her ride was nothing like my last one with that miserable man.

I walked outside into the sunshine and let the screen door slam my worries shut in the house behind it. I approached Johnny with my idea for freedom. After explaining what I wanted to do I could see the doubt on his face, so I added, "Johnny, we've got to do this, there is no other way. I think you know that too."

"That's crazy, Emily. How would we live? And we'd probably get caught. Then what?"

"Come on, Johnny. Anyplace would be better than here. And if we get caught, it couldn't really be much worse than it already is, right?"

"You're going to have to give me some time to come up with

ogot

ерж

some sort of a plan, Emily. We can't just take off in the middle of the night not knowing where we're going or what we are going to do. We need a plan. That's IF I decide to go along with you at all." He looked away from the chickens and right at me for that last sentence.

I started to protest, but he wouldn't let me. "Wait, let me finish. I don't have much longer here either way, so why should I make things worse for myself?" He went back to spreading the chicken feed around the ground as he continued, "Dad thinks I'm going to stay around and help out with the farm, but I'm not. I need to get as far away from this house and its rotten memories as I can. But I'll make a plan somehow and decide while I'm making it if I'm going to be a part of that plan or not. Now go before Mom gets suspicious or Dad gets back. And please try to stay out of trouble until I get back to you about this. You've made things pretty bad for yourself around here lately. I would hate to see you get into any more trouble."

I gave him a quick hug and said, "Thank you. I love you," then skipped back into the house while he continued with his chores outside. He hadn't said no and that was a good thing. It didn't sound like he would tell Mom or Dad what I was trying to do either. That was excellent.

Now I would just have to wait for him to come to me with a plan. I felt so hopeful and excited; it was hard to contain my joy.

I agreed that this sounded promising, but we had no idea what their father was doing right now with Caroline and what that would bring. WE would just have to wait and see where that was concerned, I guess. Having her room moved down to the cellar was just ridiculous. I couldn't believe that her parents did that to Emily and I couldn't imagine what else they might have in store for her. My time was coming soon, I could feel it.

CHAPTER ELEVEN

I purposefully slowed my step and hung my head a little as I went back into the house to ask Mom if there were any chores to be done. She would definitely be suspicious if all of a sudden I seemed happy and perky. Sometimes there would be a list of chores that needed to be done hanging on the fridge, held in place by Mom's apple magnet. There hadn't been a list since the day that we buried my little brother Eric though. So I would have to risk getting yelled at and ask.

Mom was in her room. I heard her crying before I got to the door. It was open enough to be able to see her lying across her bed, looking through some items in an old shoe box. They looked like pictures. I cleared my throat so she wouldn't think I was sneaking up on her and then pushed the door open a little wider.

Mom hurried to put the pictures or whatever they were back in the box. Then she quickly put the lid back on, wiped away her tears, and tried to sit up before I saw her. I acted like I didn't see any of it and just started talking, "I'm sorry to bother you, Mom. I wasn't sure if there was something that I should be doing or if you just wanted me to find a chore to do."

Mom cleared her throat and sniffled. "Didn't I put the list on the refrigerator?" Before I had a chance to answer, she replied to her own question with, "Oh no, I didn't. Never mind. How about cleaning that out, the refrigerator? That hasn't been done in a while. Just take everything out. You should remember how to do the rest. I'll be out in a little bit."

"Okay. Do you want me to leave your door open or shut it?" She told me to shut it. I wondered what she was looking at when I came to the door. It looked like a bunch of old photographs, but maybe I was wrong. I don't remember ever seeing any pictures in a box before, just the few that we had hanging on our living room wall. What would make her cry like that though?

I walked through the living room and into the kitchen, ready to get to work on the fridge. I was happy to have something to keep myself occupied. I filled one of our cooking pots with hot, soapy water and threw a rag from the drawer below the silverware in it. Then I emptied the contents of the refrigerator onto the table.

I was only about halfway done with my chore when I heard the engine of our truck as it pulled down our driveway towards the house. Shortly after, Caroline came bursting through the front door shouting, "Mommy, Mommy! Daddy took me for an ice cream and I made a friend while I was there! She's going to come here to spend the night in a few days! Daddy already said that she could!"

Mom had just come out from her bedroom and I saw her hold Caroline's shoulders as if to try to physically calm her down. "Okay, okay, Caroline. That's great. I can't wait to meet your new friend. Now why don't you go bring your dirty clothes down for me so that I can wash them?"

Dad was carrying a big bag to the barn. I saw him through the window above the sink. Probably a bag of feed for the animals. I knew what Mom's plan probably was. She was trying to get Caroline out of the way so she could talk to Dad privately.

Hopefully she would try to talk him out of letting Caroline's new friend spend the night at our house. Her attempt would more than likely fail, but this whole thing seemed very unusual and not at all like a good idea. Dad probably had something bad up his sleeve.

I went back to scrubbing at the crud on the side of the refrigerator, pretending not to be paying attention to what was going on around me. Caroline headed upstairs dutifully to get her dirty clothes like she was told. I was right. Mom headed past me and out the side door to confront Dad.

I could see my parents through the window as Mom approached Dad. She was already getting loud because I could hear her from where I was at and she was obviously irritated. I wished I could hear what she was actually saying to him.

She wasn't yelling long before I saw him smack her with the back of his hand. She placed her hands where he had smacked her and then he gently brushed some hair out of her face with his hand. I had never seen my father act affectionately towards anyone. It annoyed me because I knew that it was just an act. I briefly wondered how many times he had done something similar to that with my mother. After that they talked, only raising their voices every now and then. I finished my scrubbing. Nothing more was said of any of it for the rest of the day.

While in my room that night just before bed, I noticed one of the bricks in the wall was loose. I walked over to it and wiggled it until I was able to pry it free. There was a pretty big space behind where the brick belonged. I knew what would fill that empty space very nicely. A diary. I would finally be able to write down my true feelings about anything and everything and not worry that it would be found and read. Or what would happen to me if that were to happen.

I just happened to have an empty little notebook that would make a perfect diary. Notebooks, paper, pens, and pencils were always kept on hand in our house because of the homeschooling. Mom knew how I liked to write and always made sure to give me a notebook when I asked. Mom and Dad both said the supplies looked good in case someone from the State showed up to check that we were really doing what we were supposed to be. I was eager to get started on my new journal.

I'm not sure how long I stayed awake writing for, but I was lucky that my father hadn't come down to pay me a visit while I was at it. I was so absorbed in what I was writing that I may not have heard him until it was too late. All in all I had had a pretty decent day. I fell asleep hoping that Johnny would come to me with a plan of escape the next day.

Those pictures in that box, what were they and why hadn't Emily ever seen them before? I wanted to find out. Also, what happened today? Why did their father take Caroline for ice cream? That wasn't like him at all. The deal with letting Caroline talk to some other girl for long enough to form a friendship and invite her to sleep over was strange too. Something was definitely not right. He must have something bad planned somehow. Hopefully we could find out before anything happened what exactly he expected to do.

CHAPTER TWELVE

Several days, maybe a week, passed without much of anything happening. We did our schooling and our chores and enjoyed some of the nice Summer weather here and there. But, as with anytime in this house when things seemed normal and peaceful for too long, it didn't last long.

First of all, I made a point to check the calendar that was hanging in the kitchen so I could write the date on my last diary entry. Today was July 18, 1976. I was twelve years old today. Nobody had said a word about it being my birthday. Mom was normally the first to say, "Happy Birthday," to me and then the other kids did the same after they heard her. Even Dad normally said it. Also, the birthday kid normally got to choose what was for dinner and then we had cake afterwards. Mom hadn't asked what I wanted for dinner and I didn't see any evidence that she was baking or planning to bake a cake at all.

Secondly, Johnny did come to talk to me when he got a chance to do it privately, but he didn't tell me what I had wanted to hear. And no, "Happy Birthday," either. Instead he told me, "I'll work as hard and as fast as I can to get myself in a position to be able to move out."

"But what abou...," he shushed me before I could say any more.

"Let me finish. I'm not planning to let Mom or Dad know where I'm at and as soon as I'm able, I'll come for you and Caroline. Then we don't have to worry about getting caught as much. We'll have a safe place to go."

I didn't care much for the idea of having to wait an indefinite amount of time to escape, or for the fact that he was going to leave me and our little sister behind at first, but for now it was the only hope that I had to hold onto. I reluctantly agreed with Johnny that his plan was probably for the best. I still thought that we could do something to get away sooner rather than later, but he was older than I was and Caroline and I would need him if we were really going to make this getaway work. Whenever it actually happened.

Midway through the day a strange vehicle slowed at our driveway and then began pulling in. It looked like an old junker and was rusty with chipping blue paint.

I assumed whoever was in the vehicle was here to buy something from our stand, so I headed toward the road. A woman with dark blonde hair poked her head out of the driver's side window.

"Hey, excuse me. Is this where a little girl named Caroline lives?" I saw a pretty little blonde girl with braids about Caroline's age sitting in the passenger seat as I got closer. This must be the friend Caroline had made the other day: the one that was supposed to spend the night.

I should have just lied and told the lady that I didn't know anyone by that name, but I couldn't. Dad or Caroline had probably already heard the car anyways and would be out here any minute to greet our first ever house guest.

"Yes, this is Caroline's house.

You must be the people Dad and Caroline met the other day. I'm Emily, Caroline's sister."

The woman parked her dented, rusty car behind our truck in the driveway and then both she and the little girl got out. The girl appeared to be struggling, lugging a pink backpack and pillow with her.

I hated the whole idea of this poor girl spending the night at our house. I was worried about what would happen, what my father's wicked plan must be for allowing something like this in the first place.

In my mind I pictured several police cars peeling into our driveway and then taking my father away in one of their vehicles in handcuffs, just like I had seen on a show that my mother had watched on our television. I had gone into the living room to tell her something or ask her something and she had shushed me through that part. None of us kids were ever allowed to watch the television because we always had too much other stuff to do and besides, that my parents said that it would rot our growing minds, but that was alright with me. I preferred to read books. That would be such a wonderful birthday gift though, to watch my father being taken away in a police car. But what would the price have to be for the rest of us in order to get that to happen?

Caroline came running out the front door with one of the biggest smiles I had ever seen on her face. She ran right up to the new girl and gave her a big hug. My sister was just a little taller and a lot pudgier than her friend. Then they both started talking excitedly to one another. My mother came walking out, obviously less excited than my sister about our first, and hopefully last, overnight guest.

I headed back toward the house to let our mother do whatever grownup talking she had to do with the other girl's mother. I knew better than to act nosy, even if I was concerned and curious. I noticed that the other woman was quite a bit taller than my own mother and much more slender and pretty.

My father met me at the front door as I entered. "You stay away from those girls and let them have a good time together. Don't worry yourself about what they do or how they do it. I know how you like to push your ideas on these kids. You just keep your mouth shut and mind your own business while she's here. You hear me?"

"I hear you. I'll mind my own business."

"Unbelievable. He's up to something. I'm sure of it. I'm so certain that I would bet money on it. If I had any. Ooh That gives me an idea, one that will help you and your brother and sister when you finally decide to get away. You should start skimming money from the produce stand. Just a little here and there, not enough to be noticeable. And you can hide it with your diary. I love how wonderful ideas just come to me at the strangest of times," said the voice in my head. It was a fabulous idea though and one that really would help tremendously.

I had told my father that I would mind my own business. But if I happened to witness something that I thought was my business that would be altogether different. I considered the safety and well-being of my sister my business. And now I also felt responsible for this strange girl as well.

A few minutes later the two girls came clambering in the door and up the stairs to what used to be the room that I shared with my little sister. They didn't shut up the whole way and I could still hear them chattering once the door had been shut behind them.

Suddenly, I began to wonder if my father had been planning this whole thing even before he brought my sister for ice cream. Maybe he had moved my stuff and me out of my room on purpose because of whatever he had planned for this night. The thought gave me creepy goose bumps all over.

I went about doing the dusting and other various chores my mother had told me needed to be done. I liked that I had something to keep myself occupied. I had to admit that I was feeling a little jealous about Caroline being the first Fleischer child to have the privilege of having an overnight guest, or the first to have a friend for that matter. Not that I would ever want to bring a friend of mine to spend the night at this house, but I would love to have a friend that I could feel close with. Besides that, it was my birthday, not Caroline's.

There was no way that Caroline and this girl even knew for sure whether they would really click as friends. They hadn't spent enough time together yet. And I was certain that after spending one night here that girl would never want to return again. Something would happen to scare her off.

There was more chit chat at our dinner table that evening than I could ever remember there being before. My parents, Johnny, and Caroline were all playing Twenty Questions with our guest. Our guest. I realized that I didn't even know so much as the girl's name yet.

By the time I headed to the cellar for the night, I knew much more about our visitor than I had before starting dinner. Her name was Summer and she was nine years old. She would be celebrating her tenth birthday on October 2nd. She lived alone with her mother in an apartment in town. She was going into the fifth grade at Dereves Elementary in the Fall and was typically a "B" student. Her mother worked as a waitress at The Diner and they were pretty close, only having each other to lean on for everything most of the time. Her father had broken his relationship with her mother off right after she had told him that she was pregnant. He had claimed that her mother had slept around and that the baby couldn't possibly be his. Summer said that her mother told her she got her freckles from her father. All this Summer had told our whole family over dinner.

Summer was quite a talkative little girl, and did not seem too shy to share anything. She must not have learned what Johnny, Caroline, and I had about keeping quiet. After dinner the two girls went off to play and get ready for bed. I did the dishes by myself and then went down to my space in the cellar.

My twelfth birthday had come and was now gone without any mention at all from anyone. I guess I shouldn't have expected anything different after the way things had all been going around here lately. It still hurt not having anyone acknowledge what was supposed to be my special day though. I shared my feelings on the subject with my diary and then tucked it safely into its hiding place behind the brick.

Dad came down to visit after I had fallen asleep. This was his first visit to my new room. Never before had he done the bad thing on my birthday. Of course, I didn't know what time it was and maybe it wasn't even my birthday anymore. For some reason it seemed even scarier happening down here than it had in my old bedroom. Maybe because I knew in my old room if I absolutely had to scream it would wake Caroline and then he would probably stop what he was doing. It wasn't something that I had ever planned on or wanted to do, but it had at least been an option if things got too unbearable. I wasn't sure if anyone would be able to hear me from down here or if they would come to my rescue even if they did.

I didn't fight this time. I was too scared of what might happen if I did. It was pretty much the normal unwanted visit from Dad. He spit on his hand and rubbed it on my private parts to help smooth his way in. It still felt like something tore and the whole thing was just as painful as it always was. I wondered if sex was always like this no matter whether you were willing or not. If it always hurt so badly, why did women choose to do it? Maybe some women wanted a baby so bad they were willing to go through anything to get it. I didn't know and I thought if it was like that all the time, I would never do it willingly.

He finished up and left me alone in my dark cellar room. I laid there sore and thinking. If he had done the horrible thing to me, then he must not have bothered either of the other girls. At least, normally he didn't bother two of us on the same day that I was aware of. So what were his plans concerning Summer and his reasons for letting her spend the night at our house? All I knew was that I had more than one horrible feeling about this girl and the sleepover situation.

I wasn't sure why Emily's father had arranged for Summer to spend the night here but I did agree with Emily that something was definitely not right. That man was up to something awful. I only hoped it didn't involve Emily at all. I had only one thought about that. He could be trying to build trust with the girl and her mother in order to maintain a long term relationship in which to use one or both of them. That was the only reason I could think of for him to allow her to spend the night without laying a finger or any other nasty parts on her. Of course, Summer being here hadn't helped Emily escape a visit from her father.

At least I had thought up the idea of skimming money from the produce stand for Emily to save up and she seemed to like the thought. That could help out at any time whether she ran away with her brother and sister or not. Hopefully she could save quite a bit of money that way and not get caught.

Her whole family must have forgotten about Emily's birthday. Either that or Emily's parents had purposely overlooked it. Either way, her birthday meant that she was one year closer to being free of this place and her lousy excuse for parents.

CHAPTER THIRTEEN

The next day I woke and went about my normal, everyday routine of making my bed, eating breakfast, doing the dishes, and beginning the other chores that I had been given. Our school lessons for the day were forgotten about since we had a guest.

I saw Caroline and her friend as they were getting ready to hop in our pickup with Dad to take Summer home. They both seemed happy and not in the least bit upset or hurt in any way. Maybe the ride to bring her home would change that.

I wasn't hoping that it would. I just found it very strange that for the first time ever we had a young girl as a house guest, invited nonetheless by my father, and she actually seemed to have enjoyed her stay.

I decided that for now things seemed to be fine and there was nothing that I could really do even if they hadn't been. So I sauntered on out to the garden to gather some vegetables for a macaroni salad. While I was picking a cucumber, Johnny came up from behind me. "What do you think about Summer?" he asked.

"What do you mean? She seems like a nice girl to me."

He was standing next to me now. "I know that. I mean, what do you think Dad's up to?"

"Oh, that. I'm not sure, but I have a feeling it's something bad. I've had a horrible feeling about the whole thing ever since I first heard about Caroline meeting this new friend, Johnny. Do you have any ideas?"

"No. But I'm with you. I don't think anything good is going to come from this. Keep your eyes and ears peeled and I'll do the same. I had better get back to cleaning this chicken for supper before they get back."

"Okay," I said and turned my head to watch him walk away. I caught Mom watching us through the kitchen window. She moved away from it when she saw me look in her direction. I wondered if she would tell Dad that she had seen us talking with each other. Even if she did, she couldn't possibly have heard what was said and we could say that we were discussing just about anything.

I finished gathering the necessary vegetables for the macaroni salad and then took them into the house to wash and prepare them. Mom had already boiled the macaroni and had it draining in a colander in the sink.

Johnny came in with the chicken, all ready to go into a pan in the oven. Dinner was going to be delicious. At least tonight I could be certain of what we were actually eating. Mom let me finish putting the macaroni salad together. I really enjoyed cooking and I honestly didn't think she enjoyed doing much of anything anymore. If she ever did in the first place.

When it got to be around dinner time and Dad and Caroline weren't yet home, I started to get anxious. What could be happening? The unfortunate answer was: just about anything. That's what had me worried.

They arrived home while the rest of us were eating our suppers.

Caroline seemed distracted and unusually quiet. She didn't look at any of the rest of us and just ate her food. Dad, on the other hand, seemed like he was in a fairly good mood. However, I did notice that he seemed to be keeping an eye on Caroline. What had happened while they were gone, I wondered?

The next day I tried to find an opportunity to talk to Caroline alone, but no chance presented itself to talk to either one of my siblings by myself. Dad kept us all busy doing various chores. I was certain now that he was keeping an eye on my younger sister too. Something had happened yesterday while they were gone that my father didn't want the rest of us to find out about. Why else would he be keeping such a close eye on Caroline?

My diary got a full rundown of my suspicions and possible ideas about what took place on Caroline and Dad's trip to take her friend home. I would need to find a new notebook to use soon, this one was filling up awfully fast.

Dad announced at breakfast the next morning that he was going to bring me and Johnny with him on his errands. I felt comforted by the fact that Johnny would be with me, but very uneasy about why we were both supposed to accompany our father. He never took more than one of us at a time with him anymore.

When he used to take more than one of us with him, it was always the boys and that was normally for fishing trips. I highly doubted that he had a fishing trip in the day's plans for the three of us. But with my father, you never did know what to expect. Normally it wasn't good. Expect the worst and if it didn't happen, it was a pretty good day. That was how I had lived my life so far.

During our ride my father explained what exactly it was that we were expected to do and how to do it. I was seated in the middle, between my father and Johnny. I looked at Johnny. He didn't look back at me. He just continued to stare silently out the window on his side.

I had been hoping for some sort of reaction from my older brother. I was seated too close to my father to speak out myself. I supposed he could reach Johnny too from where he sat, but Johnny's chances were better than mine. We couldn't just go along with our crazy father on this. We could all get into serious trouble if we did and got caught, not to mention I would rather do just about anything other than what we were about to do.

I was certain now that Emily's father had lost his marbles if he ever had any to begin with. I didn't know how he ever thought that he would get away with what he wanted to do. To involve his two oldest children, my Emily being one of them, in his insane plan just proved how crazy and cruel he actually was. Maybe he would get caught, that would be good. I thought that even if the police knew that Caroline and Johnny had been involved, they wouldn't be punished because of the situation that they were in themselves with their father. Emily really needed to let me help her.

CHAPTER FOURTEEN

My father pulled the truck up alongside a sidewalk. I could see a playground from where I sat. I hesitated and my father urged me on by saying, "If you don't fuckin' do this, I swear I'll cut your brother's pathetic excuse for a man part off and feed it to you while he watches and bleeds to death." I couldn't be the reason that another family member of mine got murdered by this freak. So I got out of the truck and headed slowly towards the playground.

There were several children running around and screaming happily. Some were taking turns on the slide and a couple of them were swinging. One little girl was being pushed by her mother. She had to be about three years old. I felt my stomach beginning to bubble. These were the people my father had told me to approach. I let the tears roll. I had to keep in mind that I was protecting my own family.

I was blubbering as I walked up to the young lady who looked so happy pushing her daughter on the swing. She only looked a little bit older than Johnny really and she was very pretty. She had long blonde hair and was tall and thin. She was wearing makeup: blue above her eyes and pink on her lips and cheeks. She probably didn't even need the makeup to be so beautiful.

Her little girl still had her baby chunk and was adorable. She had blonde little ringlets pulled up into pigtails on the top of her head. She yelled out, "Mommy, push me higher," and then giggled, showing off a dimple on the right side of her mouth, as her mother obeyed.

Then I saw them as skeletons, the bigger one pushing the smaller, and this time the giggle sounded wicked. I shook the image from my head. The crying was good; it would make me more convincing. I just needed to do what I was told and get it over with. "Miss?"

"Yes? What's wrong?"

"I lost my puppy and I can't seem to find him anywhere. I thought I saw him run that way," I pointed toward the road where our truck was parked. "Can you please help me?"

She looked around, as if trying to find someone else to pass me and my problem off to instead. I'm sure she just wanted to continue making her sweet little daughter laugh that adorable laugh. She probably wasn't sure how to help me either. Then her daughter spoke, "Mommy, can we help her find the puppy? Please?"

"Of course we'll help. Come on Michelle." She lifted her daughter off the swing and set her on the ground. I began to notice how hot it was out and that I was actually sweating.

I lead the way towards the truck saying, "He headed this way." Everyone on the playground was busy watching their own children, playing, reading, or other things of that sort. I couldn't help feeling a little jealous. If I had ever been to such a place, it was before I could remember.

We were pretty much out of view of the other people on the playground and very near to the truck. Dad and Johnny jumped out of the truck, Dad grabbing the woman from behind and sticking his handkerchief over her nose and mouth, and Johnny grabbing the poor toddler at the same time while placing a hanky over her nose and mouth. No one was looking in our direction. My job was done. I got back into my seat in the truck.

Dad and Johnny laid our new victims in the bed of the pickup. They were sleeping for now because of something Dad had poured on the handkerchiefs. I forget what he had called the stuff.

I felt horrible for these people. More than horrible, but I didn't know what word could describe such a low, rotten feeling. I tried to shut my emotions off from the situation by telling myself that maybe this activity would keep Dad content and he would leave our family members alone for a while. I didn't know these people and I owed them nothing. Except I felt like I should at least do something to help them. Instead I had played a major role in this horror and I wasn't sure that I was done helping yet.

Dad sped away from the happy, normal people enjoying their time carefree on the playground and away from town. I was a little surprised when we pulled into our own driveway. I had expected him to drive into the middle of nowhere. That had been the original plan according to Dad. Dad would drive out to the middle of nowhere where there was a forest of trees and he and Johnny would carry the victims into the woods, tie them up, and then Johnny could return to the truck with me. Dad had said that we wouldn't be leaving the forest with our unwilling hitchhikers.

Instead of a forest, we pulled around the back of our barn, up to the big barn doors. Mom started coming out of the door on the side of the house and Dad shouted out the window of the pickup at her, "I don't need your ass out here nosing around. Stay put in the house." Then he directed his words at me, "You don't breathe a fuckin' word of this to anyone! Especially not your damn mother, hear me?"

"Yes."

He continued, "If this shit gets found out we'll all be done for. Don't forget, you're the one who tricked them to get them to the truck in the first place. And Johnny's the one who actually took that girl."

"I understand. I won't speak a word about it."

"I don't want you going in the barn for any fucking reason anymore. Make sure your sister understands that too. But don't tell her why. I'll take care of your mother. If she needs anything at all from outside the house I want you to get it for her. You can tell the bitch that much. Now go, and remember, not a goddamned word."

I headed for the house as Dad and Johnny were unloading the precious cargo of the truck. Dad lifted the young woman over his shoulder and carried her as he would carry any sack of feed. He had parked so that no one would be able to see them from the house or from the road. I could imagine what his plans were, but I preferred not to know.

I had no intention at all of telling my mother what had happened while we were away that day. Not after the way that she had reacted when I told her what our father had been doing to us kids. Or after what had happened to me afterwards because of it. For all I knew, what was taking place now might be one of the consequences of my telling Mom that day.

Emily is a very strong girl. She's certainly stronger than I gave her credit for. For her to be able to deal with the things that she has had to deal with in life so far without my help is incredible. I thought for sure today that she would need me to take over when it came to luring that little girl and her mother to the truck. She didn't though. That showed she still had more strength in her before she was truly broken by her father. Hopefully she'd never be broken by him, but I doubted that. I was certain that there would be a day soon that Emily would need me and I would be there for her, waiting to take care of things for her.

CHAPTER FIFTEEN

I walked in the door to find my mother sitting at the table. I told her what Dad had said, "If you need anything from outside, Dad wants me to get it for you."

"Yes, I need a couple of zucchinis if you guys want any dinner tonight. What's he doing out there that's so secret anyhow? Burying someone?"

I actually laughed aloud about how close she actually was to the truth with that question. "No, he's not burying anyone. He said he'd tell you what's going on when he comes in. He didn't want me to tell you. I guess he wants to tell you himself."

"Okay. Well, go get me those zucchinis. I want to make zucchini bread but I can't do it without the main ingredient."

I went back outside to do what my mother asked. I picked the zucchinis and headed back for the house. There was a woman's scream from the direction of the barn. Separating myself from that situation was going to be a lot harder than I had originally thought. I hurried the rest of the way back to the house, trying hard not to hear anything else.

I laid the vegetables on the table in front of Mom and then asked if she needed any help. She said, "No. Caroline helped me earlier. All I have left to prepare for supper is the bread and the other chores are already done. The three of you were gone for quite a long time. You can go find something to do on your own until dinner's ready."

That was easy enough. Then I remembered that I needed another notebook soon. I asked my mother, "Do you have another notebook that I can use for my stories? The other one got all wet and ruined somehow so I threw it out," I lied.

"Yes, but do you need it right this minute?" She sounded a little frustrated.
"No, whenever you get a chance to get it is fine. Thank you."

I went downstairs to my room and got my "ruined" notebook out. I wrote about the day's events and the guilt that I didn't think I'd ever be able to get rid of. And I didn't think I would ever be able to get that adorable little girl out of my head. Michelle. That's what her mother had called her. Her mother that so obviously loved and adored her. I would probably never be able to get the image of her mother smiling so lovingly while pushing her on the swing out of my head either. Why didn't I just tell the woman what my father was trying to make me do instead? I could have ran and hid from Dad and... and something. I could have done so many things differently today that didn't end with a toddler and her mommy being held prisoner in our barn.

My notebook was full. I shoved it down into the wall as far as I could and then replaced the brick. Just then I realized that I had forgotten to tell Caroline to stay in the house. I left the cellar to go find her. Hopefully she hadn't already tried to go outside. We'd both be in deep trouble if she had.

I walked quickly upstairs, trying not to seem worried. I asked Mom if she knew where Caroline was. She told me to look upstairs. I climbed the stairs that led up to Caroline's room two at a time. The room that we used to share. She was in there playing quietly with her dolls on the hardwood floor next to her bed. I walked in and closed the door behind me.

"Hey Caroline. How do you like having this big room all to yourself now?"

"I hate it Emily."

"What's wrong? What happened yesterday when you took your friend home?"

"Daddy said he'd kill me if I ever told anyone. You won't tell anyone I told you, will you?"

"No, of course not. You can always tell me anything. I told you that before. Now tell me what's bothering you." I sat on the floor next to her and held her head against me like I always used to do until just recently when our parents started trying to separate us.

"Daddy made me wait in the car while he took Summer in to her mom. He was gone a long time, so I got out of the truck and went up to their apartment to see what was taking so long." She paused to wipe snot from her nose with the sleeve of her shirt. "The door was open and I could see them both laying on the floor in a big huge puddle of blood. They were both dead Emily! Daddy killed Summer and her mom. He was on his way out when I got to the door and he yelled in a whisper for me to get back to the truck. Then on the way back home he told me that if I told anyone at all what I saw he would kill me. I don't want any more friends ever again Emily." She cried hard against my shoulder while I held her.

"I know, I know." I brushed the hair away from her face gently with my hand. "Hey, I came up here to tell you something. You have to listen. It's for your own good. Don't go outside at all for any reason unless you're told to. I can't tell you any more than that and that's for your own good too. Dad's a very bad man. I'll get you out of here soon, don't worry. Johnny and I are trying to work on a plan together to get far away from here and never have to come back." I lifted her face carefully with my hand so that our eyes met and then I said, "I love you, okay?"

"Okay Emily. I love you too. I won't go outside and I won't ask why not. I promise."

I left her room and walked back downstairs as quietly as possible, trying to hear if Dad or Johnny were back in the house yet. I didn't want to get caught by Dad leaving Caroline's bedroom right now.

Before Eric had been killed I hadn't thought that things could get any worse than they already were around here. I had been so very wrong. If our father was crazy and controlling before that night, he was a lunatic now. There wasn't anything that I could think of that he wouldn't do. In my mind, we were all in danger for our lives.

My mother and father were in their bedroom. Fighting. They weren't just screaming and hollering either. Stuff was being broken and someone (most likely my mother) was being hit. Johnny was sitting at the table by himself.

"Johnny, what are we going to do? We can't let this continue," I whispered and then looked around to make sure no one was watching us.

"What are we supposed to do? You heard Dad. We were part of this. Even if we somehow freed those two out there, they would rat us out and we'd all rot in prison or be put to death."

I wanted to run and scream and hide. This whole thing was crazy. How did we end up like this? I didn't want to be part of the kidnapping, torture, and probably murder of that cute little girl and her mommy.

Life was not fair. Didn't God exist? Why would he let something like this happen? What was the big test he must be trying to put me through? Was this a test to see if I would do the right thing and free them? I made up my mind. I would go and set them free in the middle of the night. No matter what the cost was to me and my family. I never should have taken part in the whole thing in the first place. Now I had to at least make things right.

Supper was awkward. Almost everything was always awkward in the Fleischer household. Mom looked worse than I had ever seen here before. Her whole face was swollen and bloodied. Dad seemed to be worried and keeping a close eye on each of us, as if trying to read our thoughts for anything that might be in the least bit suspicious.

Finally dinner was over, dishes were done, and all of us kids were in our rooms. I was determined to stay awake until I was sure Mom and Dad were in their bed for the night. I thought that I should be able to hear the footsteps as they went into their room. In the meantime, I had to come up with a plan. I should have told Johnny what I wanted to do and then maybe he could have helped me. But he had seemed scared about being caught by the law and what the punishment would be.

I was trying to think of who had the worse situation, me or the young woman in our barn. I really was trying to keep the little girl named Michelle out of my head. Was her mother's situation really worse than my own though? I had lived for years expecting one form of hurt or another every single day. She seemed to have lived a happy life until I walked into it.

So which was better, to live everyday worrying and wondering what would happen next or to go through life carefree until one day the unexpected happened? How long would she really have to suffer for? I was guessing a maximum of a couple of days. What would happen to me though if I interfered and got caught? The answer to that was probably many more years of unspeakable torment.

But then I thought of her sweet little daughter. That must have been torture of the most horrible kind, to have to watch whatever my father decided to do with her daughter and not be able to do anything to stop him. For myself I think that would be far worse than anything that he could possibly to do hurt me. And she was so young. Even if he never touched Michelle at all she probably had to witness whatever my father did to her mother. And that would be damaging enough.

My stomach turned. I knew in my heart that I had to do something. I just wasn't sure what yet. First I would have to go out and check out what the situation actually was that I had to deal with. If there even was anyone left alive to be dealt with. There was always the possibility that the woman and her little girl were already dead.

I hoped for Emily's sake that the strangers in the barn were already dead. Then she wouldn't have to worry about what she should or shouldn't do anymore. It would be out of her hands. There wasn't anything that she could really do for them anyway, nothing that she would be able to get away with anyhow. I wished that she would change her mind about going out to the barn at all. I had a bad feeling about what she might find, or that she would get caught.

CHAPTER SIXTEEN

I heard footsteps on the floor above me. Then I heard my father's heavier footsteps and my parents' bedroom door bang shut. Now was the time for me to act. I snuck quietly back up the basement stairs. I opened the door to the kitchen and peeked out. The lights were off and no one was in sight. My heart was racing.

I entered the kitchen and purposely didn't shut the cellar door all the way behind me. Then I tiptoed over to the door that led outside. I caught a glimpse of my reflection in the glass. I barely recognized myself and was almost afraid of the strange girl that looked back at me.

I opened the door as quickly and quietly as I could and again didn't shut it completely behind myself. I held the screen door as it shut so that it wouldn't slam. I was sure the loud beating of my heart would give me away, but also knew that was a silly thought.

I had made it outside. I crept as invisibly as I could across the damp grass. The barn seemed so far away under the present circumstances. Everything seemed so quiet. Even the crickets and other night creatures seemed to have disappeared or were holding their breaths in order to see and hear what happened next.

When I was still a little ways away from the barn I saw something that I didn't remember being there before. I sped up the last few feet until I was actually at the barn door and confirmed what I had thought. There was a chain holding the door with a padlock hanging from it. Now what? I tugged at the doors to see if they would open enough for me to fit through. They opened about two inches and made a loud dragging sound as they did so. My heart skipped a beat or two and I looked back towards the house just to make sure that no one else was headed this way.

I heard a low moaning sound coming from inside the barn. It had to be the mother. That meant that they were probably both still alive. Hopefully the little girl was sleeping. I decided to double check the other door to the barn just in case my father had left that one unlocked. I walked around the side of the barn, all the way to the other end only to find another chain and padlock. Of course, I should have known that he wouldn't leave one of the doors unlocked.

If I were going to attempt a rescue I'd need to find something to cut the chain or the lock. I was sure we had a tool that would do that sort of a thing. It would have to wait until tomorrow though. I was certain that if I spent even another minute out here I would get caught for sure. I headed quickly back to the house, feeling more nervous about sneaking back in than I had about sneaking out in the first place. If that was even possible. I opened the screen door and then pushed the inner door open. Dad was standing there, apparently waiting for me to return.

Shit. Emily had made the right decision to give up for the night and go back to the house but he had caught her anyways. What would happen to Emily now? I was so afraid for her. This was not good, not good at all. She might end up needing me sooner than I thought if things got any worse than they had been lately. What in the world was he going to do with her?

I didn't believe in praying, because I didn't believe that there was a God. If there was a God, he wouldn't have let the things that Emily's father did happen. I knew Emily believed in Him, despite the fact that her life was a living Hell, and I couldn't understand why. I knew she was more hopeful about the world and its possibilities than I was. I saw things as they were and as they needed to be changed. Tonight Emily may need something a little stronger than hope to carry her through, she may need me.

CHAPTER SEVENTEEN

Now the question running quickly through my mind was: should I just admit what I had been doing or should I make up a lie? I decided to lie. "Oh Dad, you scared me!"

"What in the hell did you think you were doing out there?"

"I was just trying to quiet that lady. I could hear her screaming all the way in my room. I didn't want someone else to hear." Would he believe me?

I barely saw his hand move before it slapped hard against my cheek. "You make a horrible liar. How stupid do you think I am? Do you want to go see how I know that you're lying to me? Do you?!"

No, I really did not want to go out into the barn and face those people. Especially not with my father when I would be able to do absolutely nothing to help them, not even to reassure them with words. Would he let me escape back to my room without going out to the barn to become a witness to whatever he had done? I really didn't think so at this point.

I tried to get out of the situation by admitting my lie but I left out the part about planning to set them free, "No, that's okay. I'm sorry. You're right, I lied to you Dad. I didn't hear the woman scream. I just wanted to go out to check on them. I just could not get to sleep knowing that they were out there."

"And just what were you planning to do so that your pretty little head would be able to get to sleep tonight? I know how you are. You think too much and are too bull headed and it's going to end up getting you into a world of trouble. So what did you think you were going to gain by going out to see them?"

"I don't know. I didn't think about it, I guess."

"Were you going to try to let them go?"

"No, Dad! Of course I wasn't going to do that."

I felt cornered. I was stuck between my father and the screen door. It would be easy enough to push the screen door open to get away, but I would never dare do that, not with a father like mine.

"Even if you did manage to free them, where would they go? Running down the road in the middle of nowhere? That woman would go right to the police you know. Then you, your brother, and I would all be put to death in the electric chair. Do you know how that would feel?"

I was looking at my feet. I began to shuffle them together as I replied to my father, "No, Sir."

He placed his rough pointer finger under my chin to lift my face towards him. Then he kept pointing the same finger right at my nose as he said, "Worse than anything you have ever experienced. Then you would go to Hell after that." Finally the pointing stopped so he could raise both of his arms in the air to show how frustrated he was with me. "I'm only looking out for what's best for you kids. That's all I ever do. You kids don't see that though."

I looked back at my feet. Wow, my father was really talkative tonight. I didn't care for it. I just wanted to go back to my room and hide. Looking out for what was best for us kids? What a bunch of bologna! I wondered if he actually believed that load of garbage himself. Probably, being the special kind of crazy that he was. I wondered if I would set him off if I just simply asked him if I could go back to bed. My stomach was bubbly again, stupid nerves.

I looked back up at my father's hands. "If it's okay with you I think I will just go to bed now."

He put that same rough pointer finger to his chin as if he were really thinking hard about this. "Hmm." The finger came off his chin and his hand flew up. I flinched, thinking that he was going to smack me again. Instead he yelled, "Now you care whether or not it's alright with me? Where was this concern about what I wanted when you was sneaking around outside so late at night?"

"I'm sorry Dad. I should have just stayed put in my room. I won't do it again, I promise."

"No, I can see that you're curious. So you can march your little ass right out with me to the barn, see what's what, and then you can come back in and go to bed. Come on, let's get out there."

I really didn't want to go out there with my father. But I could tell that he was not going to leave me alone to go to bed until I did. I was afraid of what I would find in the barn and also of what might happen to me or those people while we were out there.

Oh man, oh man, oh man! I wish Emily would just make a run for it. She could probably make it to somewhere that he wouldn't be able to find her before he could catch up to her. But I knew she wouldn't do that. She was too concerned about leaving her brother and sister. I had a really, really bad feeling about her going out to the barn with her father. I hadn't wanted her to go out there at all, but she wouldn't listen to me and now look at the position she had gotten herself into. I hoped, at the very least, that if things began to get bad she would let me take care of them for her this time.

CHAPTER EIGHTEEN

He nudged me forward out the door. The crisp night air filling my lungs and sky full of bright stars mixed with the sounds of the country night would have been breathtaking under almost any other circumstances. However, the barn and what waited inside were far too near for any sort of comfort.

I had no idea what to expect when the barn doors opened. There was a very real possibility that I would crap my own pants, that much I knew just by the way that my stomach felt all twisty and turny. I had heard the woman moaning maybe only about half an hour ago or so, so I knew that she was still alive in there. However, I hadn't heard anything at all from the little girl Michelle, that poor baby. Now I kind of hoped in the back of my mind that she was already dead only so that I wouldn't have to be a witness to any of her suffering.

The chain clattered as my father undid the lock and removed both things from the door. I was behind him on the right, trying my best to hide behind the cover of the barn door as he began to pull it open. It made such a racket as it creaked and then stuttered against the uneven ground. Our entrance shouldn't have come as a big surprise to anyone with all the noise that was made.

The smell gagged me as soon as I entered the barn. It was so bad that I swore I could taste each and every disgusting odor in my mouth. There was a mingling of human feces, vomit, sweat, urine, that nasty smell of sex, and death. I puked, adding to the nasty stink and the taste in my mouth.

The woman was moaning again, or so it sounded. Actually, her arms and legs were tied and there was something shoved in her mouth with a tie holding whatever was in her mouth in place. Her green eyes were wide in a useless attempt to show me whatever she was trying to say with her mouth.

Then I saw her beautiful little girl. Her once beautiful little girl, that is. Her body had been chopped into several smaller pieces which were lying on the work bench. I gagged some more.

My father spoke, "Now, you didn't get too attached to that little girl I hope, Caroline. I was starting to, but I got a bit carried away. All for the best, I suppose. Now I just have that one to figure out what to do with." He motioned towards Michelle's mother with his right hand without even glancing at her.

Then he looked at the older of the two people we had kidnapped and continued speaking, "Isn't that right? I can't just let you go, can I? You wouldn't want to screw up my little girl's whole future, would you? Besides, you have nothing left to live for now that your little girl is gone, poor thing." Michelle's mother struggled against her own restraints. I knew how she must have felt.

Dad spoke to me again, "Remember what I always say, Caroline? Don't get too what? Come on, you ought to know this."

He was, without a sliver of a doubt, crazy in his head. "Oh Dad, no, please!"

A wicked sound that was supposed to be a laugh escaped from his mouth. "Okay, okay. I'll finish the phrase for you. Don't get too attached because it might be supper!" He laughed again, obviously pleased at his own twisted version of what was funny.

The little girl who was once named Michelle's mother wrestled around with her restraints some more while trying without any luck to speak. Tears streamed from her eyes. I couldn't help myself. I had to say something to this poor woman. "I'm so sorry Miss. Please forgive me."

My father mimicked me in a high-pitched voice, "I'm so sorry Miss. Please won't you forgive me? Aaah, hogwash! You don't need her forgiveness! You're so fuckin' weak! Just like your pathetic, drunk mother!"

"This is wrong! You're wrong! You're out of control Dad."

He grabbed me and threw me to the dirt floor of the barn. I landed right next to the crying mother of the now dead little girl. My father quickly climbed on top of me before I had a chance to react, straddling my waist.

"You just don't know when to keep your damn trap shut, do you?" He was unfastening his pants. Once his evil man part was freed he grabbed a fistful of my hair at the back of my head. While cramming my mouth full with his penis he said, "This is what a mouth like yours deserves." He thrust his hips while also moving my head back and forth so that his thing slid quickly in and out.

It felt like his man part was choking me, reaching all the way to the back of my throat. I bit down. He quickly removed his hurt body part from my mouth.

He backhanded me and hollered, "You little bitch! So you want it rough now, do you?"

I stopped coughing and wiped my mouth. "No Dad. I'm sorry. I didn't mean to bite you. It was an accident, I swear!" I started to get to my feet but he just pushed me back down. This time I landed on the stained and dirty lap of our captive.

"No Dad! Why do you do these things?" My begging and questions weren't helping things any. He grabbed my shirt and tore it right off my body, leaving my chest open for anyone to be able to see. Then he ordered me to take off my pants. "No, please. I'll behave, I promise. I'll do whatever..."

"Take them off now like I told you to!" He already had his own clothes off and his thing was sticking straight out, almost as if saluting my father's insane behavior.

"Either way, whether you obey your father or not, this isn't going to turn out well for you at all. So why should you make things easier for him," Julie asked from inside my head. I decided she was right so I just sat there with my arms hugging my naked chest, trying to hide my developing breasts.

"Fine, I'll let you have it your way then." He walked over to the bench where the little girl's cut up body was and grabbed the butcher knife. What was he going to do? He came towards me and the now childless young woman. I squeezed myself as far back into her as I could in a useless effort to protect both of us from my wicked father.

Oh Emily, why won't you let me take over? This is horrible and it's only going to get worse from here, I have a feeling. Her father must have completely lost whatever kind of mind he had. This was all too crazy, even for the likes of him. How did he think he was going to get away with something like this? If I had my way, he most definitely would not get away with this or anything else. He also wouldn't lay another finger on Emily, ever.

CHAPTER NINETEEN

I couldn't tell which one of us he was after as he swooped in at high speed with that big knife that already had blood stains on it. Before I realized that it wasn't me, the kidnapped woman's blood was spraying everywhere, especially on me. He had sliced her throat. Her green eyes glazed over, just staring straight ahead. Dad walked back over to the bench and set his weapon down.

"Now take those pants off before I cut them off from you!"

This time I did as my father instructed. I noticed that some of the hay that was lying around the floor of the barn was quickly becoming stained with the woman's blood. I would need a bath. Her blood was all over me, on my face, my bare chest, and my arms. It had even sprayed the pants that were now falling to the dirt as I stood up.

Dad came over to me and shoved me back onto the ground. This time I landed face down in the dirt, blood, and hay. He grabbed the back of my hair again, this time pulling my head back so that I had to hold myself up on my arms. Then he lifted my waist roughly with his calf, raising my bottom in the air and bringing me to my knees so that now I was resting on all fours like some sort of an animal.

The dirt, stones, and hay from the ground dug into my boney knees. My father held my hips from behind, slamming into my private parts with his own. He forced his thing right into my girl part, not slowing or stopping to make any attempt at wetting the area to ease his way in. My hands fell out from under me from a combination of the pain and my father's force. For the moment I was positioned on my elbows.

I hoped that he would finish very soon and this night would be over. Or maybe tonight would be the night that he murdered me like he had killed Whisper, Eric, little Michelle, or her mother. As long as it was quick I didn't care. In fact, I welcomed the idea.

He yanked my head back by my hair again. Then he got off me before he did that gross thing. He kept hold of my hair and came around in front of me. "Now you're going to do this and do it right." I started to get up off the ground. "No. Stay right like you are. And if you bite me again, I promise that you won't like what happens. Open wide."

Oh God. I just wanted this awful night to end. This horrible day. This rotten life. I was exhausted from all of it: the constant worrying, thinking, being scared, the fighting, and especially this type of stuff... I just wanted it all to be over.

I heard my name being called in the distance. I recognized the voice as the one that I always heard in my head. It was the Julie voice. Was Julie really calling to me? Then I swore that I heard it again. I looked at my father to see if he had heard it as well. "Oh yes, Emily... look at me like you really want it!" He shoved deeper into my throat. I had to force myself not to puke. He obviously hadn't heard anything. Maybe I had just imagined it. Or maybe my father was just too wrapped up in the awful thing that he was doing to notice anything else. Then my father groaned loudly, pulled his thing out of my mouth in a hurry, and sprayed his nasty gooey stuff all over my face. Gross, but thank God he was finally finished.

"Oh no, stay how you are. I'm not done with you yet. In fact, we may be just getting started here." Oh God, please let this be over!

"Emily," I heard it again, a girl's voice, my Julie doll's voice. It was almost a whisper but I could definitely hear her calling my name. The Julie voice carried on, "Emily, I'm in here. Come and find me."

Who was it really and how did she know my name? Where was she and why didn't my Dad hear her talking to me? My thoughts were quickly silenced by a stinging pressure on my butthole.

"Ow, Dad, please stop! It hurts, it hurts!"

He forced his thing even harder into where poop was supposed to come out. It hurt so bad and made me feel like I had to go to the bathroom right then and there. My bottom felt like it had been ripped wide open. I was flat on my face and chest now, unable to hold myself up through the unthinkable pain. He was holding my butt in the air for himself with my thighs. When he finally pulled out of my hole I was sure the poop that was threatening to happen earlier in the night came out as well. I felt totally disgusting and couldn't wait for my bath.

"Get up, you're nasty. Go take a bath and clean yourself up. Now there's no more need for you to come out here nosing around. Our guests are gone, right?" Dad had his pants already on and was zipping them up.

"Right." My legs shook terribly as I stood and diarrhea ran down my leg.

My father reached above him and grabbed one of the green, rough emergency blankets from the loft. Handing it out towards me he said, "Here, just wrap this around you. You're too disgusting to put your clothes on even. No one should be up yet in the house. If they are just tell them to go back to bed and mind their own business."

I took the blanket, wrapped it around my naked, shaking body and began to grab my clothes from the ground.

"Are you stupid? Just leave them. They'll have to be burned."

I left my clothes where they were and finally headed out the barn door. My father stayed behind in the barn. The fresh air hit my face and traveled soothingly through my mouth and nose. I just stood there for a moment trying to breathe in as much of it as I could.

I opened my eyes back up and noticed that the sun was just starting to peek over the horizon. There wouldn't be much time for me to bathe before everyone in the house started to wake up. I hurried the rest of the way to the house and went inside. No one greeted me at the door this time around, thank goodness. I went into the bathroom. I locked the door and the nightmarish events of the night along with it behind me.

I was so close tonight, so close. I still wasn't close enough for her to embrace me and let me have the control I needed. I was beginning to wonder if Emily would ever let me take control. I had been certain that she would need help in the barn and that she would be more than willing to receive it. The only thing I seemed to accomplish was confusing her even more. I didn't want to confuse Emily or make things harder for her, I only wanted to help. I wanted to shield her from the hurt and the pain. I wanted to make it all go away for her forever. Would she ever let me?

118

CHAPTER TWENTY

I had no idea what time of day it might be when I awoke. I was more sore than I could ever remember being in my life, everywhere on my body. My eyes stung as I opened them. My bottom hurt when I sat up.

In fact, I couldn't sit correctly at all. It felt like there was a lump between my butt cheeks. I reached my hand back and gently felt around my bottom to investigate. I couldn't tell for certain, but it kind of felt like my butthole was all swollen and sticking out. I became even more scared when I realized that it was about the size of a doughnut. Hopefully the swelling would go down quickly and my butt would be normal again. I was terrified of what it would feel like the next time I had to go number two.

One thing that I didn't have to worry about today (well, actually two people that I didn't have to worry about) was what I should, would, or could do about the situation going on in the barn. There was no longer a situation. Our kidnapped guests were both dead. At least they weren't suffering any longer. According to Dad though, at least one of our guests would be joining us at the dinner table... as the main course. I wondered if I would know when that was so that I could avoid eating on that particular night. Hopefully, I would.

I heard footsteps on the floor above me. I figured that I had better get dressed and get upstairs to face whatever the day had to bring. I almost wished that I could just stay down in my room for at least a few more hours to write in my diary and just be by myself. But eventually someone would be down looking for me. I decided I'd rather show my face upstairs before that happened.

My mother and Caroline were both in the kitchen and only looked at me briefly as I entered. Caroline was washing dishes and gave me a quick smile before continuing what she had been doing. Mom was cutting vegetables... potatoes, carrots, and onions.

I heard an unfamiliar man's voice speaking with Dad in the living room. "Who's here," I whispered to my mother.

"Not that it's any of your business, young lady, but it's The Law. Apparently there have been some frightening things happening in town and the police are just checking out all the houses from what I understand. Not my business or my concern though and it shouldn't be yours either. Now get something to eat and sit down at the table."

Wow. What did this mean for us? Were they really here just because they were going house to house or were they on to my father? My head was spinning. What would happen? Would we all be in trouble or just my father? It would be perfect if they arrested my father and either locked him away for life or put him to death for his crimes. Truly wonderful. I had to keep myself from physically trying to get closer to hear what was being said.

"What time is it," I asked to try to get a better idea of what I should grab to eat. I was so hungry that I felt like I could actually eat a whole chicken myself, that much I couldn't ignore.

My mother responded without any hint of an attitude, "It happens to be four o'clock in the afternoon, sleepyhead. I made you a plate. It's in the refrigerator."

I opened the fridge to find a neatly wrapped plate of food. My father's voice got louder and angrier in the living room, "This is an invasion of my privacy! If you must, let's get this over with!"

The front door slammed shut and it was quiet in the living room now. Through the kitchen window I could see that Johnny was working out by the barn feeding the animals. I took my time getting my plate from the refrigerator and moving to the table. I saw the police officer follow my father into the barn with all of its nasty secrets ready to tell. I sat down carefully at my spot at the table mindful of my hurting bottom and began to remove my plate from its wrapping, feeling almost giddy with excitement about what might happen next.

My lunch looked so delicious. There was a turkey sandwich with lettuce and sliced tomatoes, a pickle cut in half length wise, and even a peach sliced up neatly. What a rare treat to have someone take such care to make only me a meal that I wasn't even awake yet for.

I was chewing the last bite of my wonderful turkey sandwich and really enjoying the way that the different flavors mixed together in my mouth when my sister simply said, "Oh no," to something that she had seen while looking out the kitchen window.

My mouth was full and besides that, my mother had told me to mind my own business. So I just continued to chew my food, extremely curious about what my sister had seen.

Mom was clearly upset. She sighed loudly, placed her knife down on the table and got up from her chair. "What is it Caroline?"

"Daddy is running…"

Oh, if only this would go the way that Emily and I were both hoping that it would. I had a feeling that it wouldn't. Why would her father be running and by himself? Was the cop chasing him?

Maybe this could go the way that we were hoping and then the nightmare would be over.

CHAPTER TWENTY-ONE

Our father burst through the screen door before my sister had a chance to finish telling us what she had seen. Dad actually looked nervous or scared. Maybe he was both. And he was covered in blood. It was on his hands, his clothing, and there was even a little on his face.

"What in God's name happened out there John," my mother screamed at my father, obviously shocked by his all too guilty condition.

"I killed that goddamned nosy pig of a cop. Do not look at me like that Ruth. You have no fucking clue. None at all. I'm gonna wash myself up fast. Emily, I want you to take my clothes after I throw them out in the hall. I want you to burn them out on the burn pile. Take some of the other garbage that needs to be burned too so the clothes aren't the only things on there."

A car engine roared to life outside. "What's that now," my

mother asked in a tone that implied that what was already happening was more than enough for her.

My father was already in the bathroom. He hollered out, "I told Johnny to get rid of that pig's car. Don't worry, I told him exactly where to take it and what to do." It sounded as if he had left the door to the bathroom open. "Okay Emily, come get these clothes!"

I moved quickly to obey. Being slow on my part could have easily set my father's temper off. I gathered his clothes and shoved them into the paper bag that my mother had already given me with our other burnable garbage in it. I grabbed the box of matches from the windowsill before heading through the screen door to go outside.

As I watched my father's clothes being swallowed by the hungry flames I couldn't help but wish that he were still in them, burning as well. That whole thing with the police officer had not gone as I had hoped one bit. I would have never expected my father to kill the guy though. I wasn't sure why not. His murdered victims totaled six now; not including our furry family members, unless there were others that I didn't even know about.

The evidence of my father's latest murder was now unrecognizable. Turning to walk back towards the house, I saw my father come through the screen door carrying a bucket that was sloshing something out of its sides. He shouted to me, "Emily, get over here!"

I ran to meet up with him. Once I was close enough so that he didn't have to shout he began speaking again, "I need you to help me clean the barn out. We can't leave even one drop of blood in there to be found. This is life or death important. Hear me?"

"Yes Dad, I do."

"Okay good. You can get started gathering the stained hay and bringing it to the burn pile while it's still going and I'll get rid of the cop's body. Now get moving!"

I could hear the worried excitement in his voice as he spoke. I knew what it would mean for him if he got caught. That part did not bother me one bit at all. What did worry me was whether or not Johnny and I would be in trouble along with him. I highly doubted that my father would take the fall all by himself. I had better get busy and do an excellent job of cleaning up anything that would give away any clues about what had happened here.

The stink inside the barn was unbearable. My delicious lunch came right back up and left the same way that it had gone in. It wasn't so tasty the second time through. Wonderful. It was just one more disgusting mess for me to have to clean up plus now I had the nasty taste of puke in my mouth. I looked around the barn. The only body to be found was that of the police officer. He had a pitchfork sticking out of his plump face.

I wondered what my father had done with the other two bodies, more than a little afraid of what the answer might be. I could still see where the woman's body had been sitting against one of the beams, blood everywhere around it. My own accident from the night before was still lying there as well. I started to gather the telling hay, wishing that Caroline were out here to help me with this nasty chore.

Dad entered the barn the same way that I had, carrying his full bucket. He set it down and then grabbed a couple of the burlap sacks from the pile in the loft. I headed for the burn pile with my wheelbarrow full of dirty hay, enjoying each and every breath of fresh air.

I kept in mind that my father expected the work to go as quickly as humanly possible and maybe even faster than that. I threw the hay by handfuls on the fire, making it flare up all over again. Then I made my way as quickly as I could without running back to the horrid barn where nightmares really had come true.

My father had left the barn with his newest body before I returned. I grabbed the shovel and scooped as much of the nastiness as I could up from the ground of the barn into the wheelbarrow. Hmm, where should I dump it? I decided that the place that made the most sense to dump and hide the mess would be the same place that my brother always brought the mulch that he cleaned from all of the animals- to the mulch pile.

I added my mixture of vomit, feces, and whatever else I had scooped up to the rotting vegetables, animal dung, and other household garbage that would eventually turn into soil. Then I used the shovel as I had seen both my father and my older brother do to stir the mixture so that no one would be able to tell the new from the old. The muscles in my arms burned from being used so much lately in ways that they had never really been used for that often. I hoped that Johnny would be home soon to finish helping me cover up for the messes that were made because of my father.

Back to the barn I headed once again with the wheelbarrow. Once inside I looked around for anything else big that could count as evidence against my father. I should have purposely left something to be found, but I didn't dare in case it was my father who happened to find it.

I figured it was time to start scrubbing the beams that were stained with blood. I grabbed the sponge from the bucket, leaving it dripping with hot water and soap suds. While I scrubbed I thought to myself. I wondered if these bodies would be the last to be tortured and murdered in this barn. Also I wondered if this would be the last time I had to clean up after my father had killed someone. If not, how many more times would there be and for how long would I continue to do his dirty work?

Ugh, I was worn out, sore, exhausted and hungry. My father had never returned after he had left, most likely with the body of the cop. Would there be yet another area I had to scrub clean of blood? I really, really hoped not.

I also wondered whether Johnny had ever returned from getting rid of the cop's vehicle. If he was smart he would never return. If he thought anything of Caroline and me though, he would come for us like he had told me he would as soon as he had things all set up and ready for us.

I got up, stretched, and looked around the barn carefully for any more possible evidence that I may have missed. I grabbed the broom and swept over the ground to help cover any spots where fluids had soaked in. Then I took some clean hay from one of the bales sitting against the wall and scattered a layer over the bare ground. I wished that my father would come back out to let me know whether or not the job I had done was good enough for his liking.

Deciding not to wait around, I left the barn to go back to the house, leaving the door open on purpose to let some of the smell air out. The sun was starting to set, meaning that it was most likely after eight o'clock at night.

My mother and Emily were seated at the table in the kitchen. I asked where Dad was. Apparently he had decided to go pick Johnny up from wherever it was that he had sent him to get rid of the cop's car.

"Grab a bowl of stew and sit down with us Emily. In fact, dish me out a bowl too. This whole thing has had me so nervous I haven't been able to eat. Now I think I can stomach some. It smells good anyhow. Caroline do you want some supper now too?"

"Yes Mommy. Emily…"

"Yes, I'll dish yours too Caroline. You want some bread?" I looked at each of them, waiting for an answer. We always ate bread with our stew; I don't know what made me ask this time. Of course, yes, they both let me know that they would like some bread.

I looked carefully at the meat as I dished each bowl. I could tell that it wasn't beef or deer. It was some sort of white meat. Please God, let it be chicken. I was much too hungry to skip dinner so I made up my mind that chicken was what was in the stew. I knew that I was probably lying to myself, even as I was still making up the lie in my head.

After I had given my mother and sister their bowls, spoons, and buttered bread I sat down at the table with my own bowl of stew. I tried to make conversation to keep my mind from thinking about what I was quite possibly eating, knowing full well that I was breaking the rules of the table. "So what did you two do today?" I placed my first spoonful into my mouth.

Caroline answered first, "We cleaned the house." Then she stuck her second spoonful into her mouth.

Mom added, "We got a lot done. We did all the dusting, sweeping, mopping, and even cleaned the walls in the living room." Headlights shone through the darkness in the living room just then, shining in the mirror on the hutch that stood just outside the kitchen. "Oh good, it looks like your father and brother made it back home finally."

Dad came walking into the kitchen first followed by a gloomy looking Johnny. "Mmm, smells great," my father said as he took his seat at the table.

Mom got up from her chair and told Johnny to take a seat at the table while she dished his and my father's suppers. He took his seat, like he was told to do, looking as if he were avoiding eye contact with everyone.

I wondered what all might have happened while he was gone today. Or maybe something bad had happened before he had ever left even. I never actually saw him face to face after I woke up until just now, so it was possible. Anything was possible in the Fleischer house.

I finished my bowl of stew and got busy washing the dishes. Dad asked me if I had finished cleaning up the barn and I told him that I had.

"Good. Everything should be fine then. Nothing happened here. That cop stopped by, asked if we had seen anything strange lately and we told him no, and then he went on his merry way. That's the story if anyone at all asks. Are we all clear?"

Everyone agreed that they understood and agreed with what my father had said. They all finished eating and I finished up the dishes. Then Johnny, Caroline, and I each went to our rooms. Thank God another day was finally over and done with.

I was so very disappointed by the events of the day. There was still a good chance that their father would get caught for his crimes though and I really hoped that he did. A girl Emily's age shouldn't have to do the things that she had to do today. No girl of any age should ever have to do things of that sort.

CHAPTER TWENTY-TWO

I wrote everything about the past couple of days down in my diary. Every little bit that I could remember so that I would have it on paper. If I didn't live through growing up with my rotten father I imagined someone finding my diaries in the wall someday and sending them off to a publisher. I would be dead, which wasn't really a big deal, but I would be a famous author, which was a very big deal to me.

I even added to my diary the part about hearing someone calling my name. Before I realized what I was writing I scribbled, "In my head I knew it was Julie calling my name but I refused to believe it at the time. She wanted to hide me inside my own mind but I just wasn't ready yet."

I looked back at what I had just written, shocked and more than a little freaked out by what I saw there. No! Could that be true? But it must be. I had written it myself and it did make sense to me, in a crazy sort of way.

I threw my diary and pen back into their hiding place behind the brick as if they were a poisonous snake ready to strike out at me. After I replaced the brick I looked at my doll. "Julie, was that really you who was calling to me last night?" My lifeless doll did not reply. Of course she didn't reply. She was only a doll for God's sake! Maybe I had made the whole thing up last night because I had been so tired and stressed out. What I had written tonight could be easily explained by an overactive and overtired imagination.

I changed into my nightgown. My bed felt extra comfortable tonight, even though I had only woken up at four o'clock this afternoon. I cuddled Julie close to me and said, "I love you either way Julie. Good night." Then I said my usual bedtime prayer. I switched my brain to the off position and drifted quickly off to sleep.

Ghosts floated through my dreams. They were looking accusingly at me and pointing their fingers. They were all there: the mom that I never learned the name of, the little girl named Michelle, my little brother Eric, Lucky, and Whisper.

There were others too, but I had never seen them before. There was a man and a woman, an older girl, and another man and woman. They each seemed strangely familiar to me, though I knew for certain that I had never met any of them before in my life. And in my dream I recalled the day that I caught my mother crying in her room and thought she was probably looking at old photographs. Somehow, though it seemed nuts, I just knew that I would see my ghostly visitors in those pictures my mom had been crying over.

When I woke up in the morning I remembered my dream right away. My curiosity was going at full speed all over again. I had to find out what my mother had been looking at that day. Maybe it would answer some of the questions I had about other family and why we kids knew nothing about them. The more that I thought about it, the more sure I became that I needed to see those pictures or whatever my mother had been looking at that day.

I got dressed and made my bed as usual, wondering what the

point was of making my bed every single day. It wasn't as if anyone at all besides me saw my bed when I wasn't in it.

What was the point of anything that we did around here? We spent all day learning, cleaning, taking care of the animals and farm, and preparing and eating food. And all of it was for what reason, to live? What kind of a life was that? I knew what the reason was: to be around for my father's sick fun. If he kept up the murdering he was doing there would be none of us left. The world would be better off without the Fleischer family in it anyhow.

Letting out a long sigh, I figured it was time to show my face upstairs and headed up to do just that. My mother and father were sitting at the kitchen table eating breakfast. Caroline was just coming into the kitchen too, looking like she had just woken up herself. There was already one dirty plate and cup on the counter so I figured that Johnny must have eaten and started his chores already. The smell of the food on the stove made my mouth water.

I wondered what the day held in store for me and the rest of my family. I grabbed myself and Caroline each a plate from the cupboard and a set of silverware from the drawer next to the sink. I set her plate and silverware down on the counter next to the stove and started to make my own plate. There were scrambled eggs, sausage, and toast already made and sitting in the pan. Caroline came up behind me, took her plate and started adding her food to it. I sat down to eat just before she did.

Dad was still had food in his mouth when he started talking to us, "I think we're going to do something a little special today." He seemed to really think hard about what he was going to say next and then finally added, "Yes, I think we are. I want you both to come outside when you're through eating your breakfasts."

"Okay," I said after I had finished chewing the food that was in my mouth. I knew he wouldn't let me get away with speaking with a mouth full of food. It kind of made me angry that he didn't bother to follow his own rules. I wondered what this was all about, what this something a little special could possibly be that we would all be doing. I was still sore and swollen from the last thing my father decided to do with me. I didn't look at Caroline because I was scared that I would make a face and that Dad would see it. I was hoping to get a chance to snoop in my parents' bedroom soon, maybe even today if I could.

Dad finished his breakfast and went outside before the rest of us. Caroline and I both finished our breakfasts and then she offered to help me with the dishes. Mom headed outside. I wondered if I should dare try to sneak into their room now to find what I was looking for. I was scared, but how many chances did I really get to look in their room for something? The answer was: not very many at all.

I would try it. "Caroline, will you do me a huge favor?"

She was rinsing the plate that I had just washed. "Sure Emily. What is it?"

"Will you finish up the dishes for me and keep a look out for Mom or Dad to come back to the house? Like cough really loud if you see them heading this way. Do you think you can do that?"

She set the plate in the strainer to dry a little and then turned to face me. She looked nervous. "I don't know Emily. What are you gonna do anyways? What if you get caught? We'll both be dead meat."

"We won't get caught if you keep a good enough look out and cough like I told you. Please do this? I have to be quick. Come on Caroline," I was almost begging her, "I'll take the blame if we get caught somehow, I promise."

She turned back around to wash another plate. "Okay, I guess. Hurry up and be careful though." I kissed her on the cheek and ran off as lightly as I could in the direction of Mom and Dad's room.

Now where would Mom keep that box? I was guessing probably either under the bed or in the closet. I looked under the bed first.

There I found nothing but old magazines with naked women on the covers. I looked in the closet. It was packed full of hanging clothes and boxes of all shapes and sizes.

I looked for the box that I had seen on their bed that day. I found one that might be it, looked inside, and saw a pile of old photographs. That was lucky! I had found the box that I was looking for on the first try. I closed the lid and headed for the door with my treasure.

Caroline started coughing. Crap! I quickly left my parents' room and ran for the cellar door. I heard the screen door begin to open and darted into the bathroom with the dusty box instead. My heart was pounding.

I heard my mother's voice and relaxed just a little knowing that at least it wasn't my father in the house. "Where did Emily take off to," I heard her ask my little sister.

"I'm not sure Mommy. She ran off in a hurry. Maybe she had to use the bathroom." She coughed again loudly.

"Are you alright," my mother was still in the kitchen talking to Caroline. I turned on the water in the sink and locked the bathroom door. After a few moments there was a knock.

"Yes," I replied to the knocker that I knew must be my mother.

"Are you okay," she asked loudly to make sure I could hear her over the running water and through the door.

"Yes. My stomach was just upset and I had to go to the bathroom. I'll be out in a couple of minutes." How would I know when she went back outside?

"Okay, well your father is waiting on you girls so hurry it up before he gets mad."

"I'll try Mom," and I turned off the faucet on the sink so I'd be able to hear the sounds outside of the bathroom better. A few moments later I heard her tell my sister to hurry up and get outside with or without me and then the screen door slammed shut.

I opened the bathroom door a crack and peeked out. No one was around except my sister. Good. I ran to the cellar door with my mother's box and then shut it behind me again as I rushed down to my bedroom. I quickly shoved the box under the clothes in my nightstand and ran back upstairs.

Caroline had just finished putting the last of the clean dishes away. "Okay, thank you so much. I owe you one. Let's go out to see what Dad wants now."

I didn't know what to think of the box of pictures that Emily now had hidden in her bedroom. She would be in so much trouble if she got caught with them and I was afraid for her. I was also a little curious to see what was inside the box and to see if the people Emily had seen in her dream would really be in the photos or not. Emily had some of their features so I was thinking that they could be relatives of hers.

I was also wondering what her father wanted her and her sister outside for so badly. Whatever it was that he wanted them for, I was sure it was nothing good.

CHAPTER TWENTY-THREE

Dad, Mom, and Johnny were all out near the cooking pit just behind the house. What were they doing there? There was smoke rising from the pit and Dad was holding what looked like his poker in the coals. What in the world were we going to do? I couldn't guess the answer to that for the life of me.

Caroline and I joined the rest of our family at the cooking pit. Mom seemed excited about what we were going to do. Did she know already? Dad acted excited too. He pulled his branding iron out from the hot coals.

"Alrighty Ruth, you're first," he was speaking to my mother, "Let's see that butt!"

What the heck?! He was going to brand us?! I looked at Johnny who appeared to already have known what was going to take place out here and then at Caroline who looked as scared and horrified as I felt.

"It's just like a tattoo," my father said to all of us as if we were all afraid for no reason whatsoever. "We're all going to get a family branding. It will be great!" This was a man who had lost every single last marble there had ever been in his head. I was certain of that.

My mother had made a face that said she was in pain as the hot brand met her bare bottom. I could hear her skin sizzle as the mark of the "F" was being burned into her pale flesh. Next was Johnny's turn. He yelled out in pain only once as the one inch "F" was burned into his bare butt cheek. My turn would be right after his. I was terrified.

I stepped closer to the grill, faced away from my father, and pulled my pants down just enough to show one of my butt cheeks. The swelling around butt hole was just starting to go back to normal again and I didn't want anyone to happen to see any trace of what my father had done to me out in the barn the other night.

The pain of being branded by my father was worse than I had been expecting. I screamed out. It felt like he had burned me all the way down to the bone and it seemed to last for longer than what he had taken to brand my mother and my older brother. When he finally removed the branding iron from my bottom it felt like some of my skin must have come off with it. Tears of pain were streaming down my cheeks. I wiped them away with the back of my hand, pulled my pants back up carefully over my permanently scarred butt and went back over to stand next to my brother.

Now it was my poor little sister Caroline's turn. I knew she would scream and cry and that I would probably cry for her. She pulled her pants down below her round bottom and whined a little bit to my father about being afraid of getting burned.

My father yelled at her, "Everyone else did it without complaining. You're the last one to go. Don't be a big baby." He had my mother hold Caroline still while he placed the burning hot iron on the cheek of her bottom.

It was horrible. Caroline wailed out a scream like I had never heard from her before. Just as I had thought they would, angry, sympathetic tears flowed from my eyes. I swiped at them with my hand and looked to my right at Johnny. I could tell that he had his jaw clenched tightly shut. He was angry and trying hard not to show his emotions.

I was furious myself. I couldn't believe that our mother was allowing this. But she seemed just as excited as my father about the idea of us all being branded with the Fleischer "F". Maybe she was a lot more messed up in the head than I had originally thought. She would have to be to not only allow such torture of her own flesh and blood, but to watch and participate as well.

Being branded by our father was our "something a little special" that Dad had thought up for us to do as a family today. Hopefully our family fun was over with for the day. I didn't think that I could handle any more of my father's idea of fun today.

My bottom was stinging and burning where the new "F" now sat. My father must have had the same thought just then because he told my mother to rub some aloe from her plant on each of our new brandings. I didn't want her touching my butt, but I knew that it would help to make it feel better and I welcomed that idea.

I was really beginning to get angry. Emily needed me so much, why didn't she just let me help her? I knew she was wrestling with the idea of me and what I might mean in her mind. Soon there would be a time that she needed me and didn't care what it might or might not mean for her sanity. I was trying to save her mind for her, not ruin it.

CHAPTER TWENTY-FOUR

Our family fun was not over as I had hoped that it would be after we had all gotten our butts branded. However, we would wait to continue our family bonding time much later on, after bedtime. We spent most of the rest of the day doing different chores as was usual, spent about an hour on school work, then we ate supper, and then headed our separate ways for bed.

My journal got a full rundown of my branding experience. One thing that I realized and noted as I was remembering the events on paper was that my father did not get branded himself. He only branded the rest of us as if we were his property and might get stolen or try to run away from him. I wrote my first ever swear word that night, calling my father "one sick bastard" in my journal.

I didn't even have a chance to fall asleep. I heard the door to the cellar open and my father's heavy footsteps coming down the stairs. Not tonight, please, I thought to myself as hard as I could, thinking that maybe if I thought it hard enough it might make it come true.

I completely missed hearing the second set of footsteps as they followed my father's down the stairs. I didn't even realize he was there until I saw my older brother Johnny walk in behind our father. Good, I thought. Then he must not be down here for what I had been so afraid of only a moment ago.

My father approached me where I lay on my bed. To my surprise he ordered me to take off my panties. Why did he bring Johnny with him then if he was just going to do the bad stuff to me? I didn't understand and I really didn't like it. The stuff that he did was horrible enough without having someone there that I cared about to see it. At least when Caroline was around in my old room she was sleeping, or I thought that she was and that made all the difference to me.

I guess that I didn't move quickly enough for Dad. He reached down and yanked my underwear down my legs and off from me before I had the chance to argue and do it myself. He told Johnny to take his long underwear off. What was going on? What was he going to make us do? I hated this... probably more than anything I had been through before this, I thought.

Unfortunately, my questions were soon answered. My brother didn't look at me and I couldn't look at him either. Dad made me put Johnny's thing in my mouth and move it in and out like he had forced me to do with him. Johnny tried to argue for the both of us but Dad backhanded him across the face. That settled that discussion.

Meanwhile my father did his own painful thing down in my private girl part. I didn't bite Johnny like I had bit my father. I knew he hated this as much as I did so I was as gentle as I possibly could be while my father was shaking me with his rhythmic motion.

My brother tried to pull away from my mouth and warned me to stop what I was doing. My father, busy doing what he was doing to my girl parts but not too busy to have seen the looks between Johnny and me, simply panted, "No, don't you dare stop. It's fine Johnny.

It's only human nature. Go ahead and do it." Some tobacco stained saliva slid out from the corner of his mouth. It landed on my bed. I was grateful that it hadn't landed on me instead.

Not only did my father seem to think what was going on was fine, but he seemed to completely enjoy it and what was most likely about to happen. I knew it wasn't Johnny's fault and that he probably couldn't help it. Johnny moaned and his stuff squirted down the back of my throat.

Immediately after that my father did the same nasty thing down in my sore and swollen girl part. I gagged and then puked over the side of my bed. Hopefully this was the last thing that my father had planned out for us tonight. That was horrible and embarrassing enough for both me and Johnny.

"Clean up your mess, you nasty slob," he said to me while pointing at the vomit on the ground of the cellar next to my bed. "You go get some sleep Johnny. We have a long day ahead of us tomorrow," and then he spit his chewed up tobacco out onto the ground right next to my puke. He had some nerve calling me the nasty slob.

While I cleaned up my mess and my father's spit off the ground with my towel I wondered what my dear old dad had planned for the following day. Knowing him, it was nothing good. His craziness seemed to have taken on a whole new meaning and was reaching new heights since Eric's death and I didn't have any idea what limit there was to it now. There didn't appear to be any sort of limit at all to what he would do for his own twisted sense of fun and pleasure. We kids had to get out of here and fast or make my father disappear somehow.

Hmm, I would have to keep that in mind and consider that last option some more. Finally Emily was starting to think a little more along the lines that I was thinking. The way I saw things, escaping or getting rid of the problem was not a choice, one of the two things was something that just had to be done.

CHAPTER TWENTY-FIVE

When I woke up the next morning I realized that I had completely forgotten about the box I had taken from my parents' bedroom the day before. That was actually probably a good thing since I had just happened to put my journal away before my father had come downstairs with my brother. I would have gotten caught for sure going through that box of pictures.

Now would be the perfect time to take at least a quick look through it. Unless there was something really important going on no one usually bothered with me in the morning until I showed my face upstairs. I was pretty sure it was still morning. It just seemed as if it must be to me.

I got all dressed and ready for the day just in case I needed to head upstairs quickly for some reason. The whole time while I was getting ready I had the images of my unknown ghost visitors running through my mind. I was sure that I would recognize any one of them if I saw them in one of the photos in the box.

After I was completely ready to run upstairs if need be I pulled out the mysterious box full of pictures I had never seen before in my life that I had caught my mother crying over. I decided to only take a handful of the photos out and leave the box hiding where I had it.

I would have to look for a better hiding spot too if I was going to keep the box much longer. I would keep my eyes peeled and move it today when I had the chance. I wasn't sure how often my mother took it out to look through it. I was pretty certain that my dad didn't bother with such things, definitely not any more even if he once did.

According to what Dad had said to Johnny last night, they should be busy for most of the day doing whatever it was that Dad had in mind. That was okay with me for the moment. I was feeling a little ashamed about what took place the night before and was nervous about the first time that I would have to look at Johnny again. Of course I knew that it was all my father's fault, but that still didn't erase my feelings of embarrassment about the whole thing.

I climbed onto my bed and got as comfortable as I possibly could with a newly branded bottom, still slightly swollen butthole, and freshly bruised girl part. I started to rummage through the pile of old pictures on my bed. The first thing of interest that I came upon was not a photograph, however.

There was an old newspaper clipping in along with the pictures. The headline on the article caught my eye: Man, Wife, And Young Daughter Murdered in Own Home in Dereves Overnight. I read the article as quickly as I could to find out any possible details.

"Henry J. Fleischer- seventy-two, his wife fifty-three-year-old Emma C. Fleischer, and their eleven-year-old daughter Anne B. Fleischer were all stabbed to death in their home in the town of Dereves on Tuesday night.

Their surviving son, eighteen-year-old John Fleischer, reportedly heard screams from his parents' bedroom just after midnight and ran downstairs to find an intruder fleeing from the scene. He then found the bodies of both of his parents in their bed and his youngest sister on the floor next to their bed.

Also surviving is Henry and Emma's sixteen-year-old daughter Ruth Fleischer. Evidently the intruder didn't realize that there was an attic in the home where the children had bedrooms, ultimately saving their lives.

Investigators are still working hard and looking for any leads to find the murderer. Please contact the town of Dereves Sheriff's Department at 555-238-9874 if you have any information you think might be helpful in this tragic incident."

Oh my dear God! Mom and Dad weren't husband and wife... they were brother and sister! Also, I would have bet almost anything that their parents' murder was not committed by some strange intruder. This must have been why we never heard anything about our other family members or about Mom and Dad's childhood. And this was the house they both grew up in... Johnny's and Caroline's bedrooms were Mom and Dad's when they were younger.

My head was spinning. There was too much for my mind to figure out going on here. I heard someone open the cellar door. I scrambled to put the pictures and article back in the hidden box, not even wanting them on my bed any longer.

I would return the box today as soon as I had the chance. I didn't need to see any of the pictures, not anytime soon. The one ghost couple in my nightmare must have been my grandparents and the little girl I was guessing must have been my aunt. I still didn't know who the other ghost couple was, but that question would have to stay a mystery for the time being. I wasn't ready to find out any more family history right now.

I wondered why my father would kill his littlest sister and not my mother. If he were going to keep one sister alive, why not let both live? I left my room and headed for the stairs. My mother was almost to the bottom with a basket full of dirty clothes in her arms.

"Good morning Emily. Breakfast is still on the stove for you. Go eat so you can help me get this house in shape today."

I moved out of her way so that she could get over to the washing machine and then I walked up the stairs and into the kitchen. I had so many new questions that I couldn't ask anyone. I wondered if I should keep what I found out to myself or tell my brother about it. I decided it would be best to keep it to myself for now.

I didn't know what to think. That article told a couple of very big, deep, dark secrets. Emily's guesses about what had really happened were probably all too true too. I wondered if Emily's grandfather had been the same sort of monster that her father was or if he had been just a nice, normal guy who happened to have an evil son.

Also, to kill his little sister was terrible... unless he hadn't been the one to do that. It really could have been anyone in the house: Emily's grandfather, grandmother, mother, or her father. Maybe that was what had set Emily's father off in the first place. Maybe he had heard sounds from downstairs and found his little sister murdered by one of his parents... who knew. I wondered if those questions would ever be answered. Either way, it didn't excuse the type of monster that her father was now.

CHAPTER TWENTY-SIX

Breakfast was the usual eggs and toast. There was sausage this morning as well. Caroline was still sitting at the table with her plate and chewing, though hers was just about gone already with only what I guessed to be one bite of egg and two bites of toast left.

"Morning. Where's Dad and Johnny," I asked as I placed two eggs on my plate with the flipper.

"I don't know. They were already gone when I got up. But Mommy said we might go to the State Fair this week Emily!" She was super excited, jumping up from the table as soon as the last bite went into her mouth. She hugged me tightly while she was still chewing. Then she brought her plate over to the sink, where three other plates already sat dirty with egg yolk, toast crumbs, and sausage grease.

I really wanted to feel excited too, but I couldn't. We had never been to The Fair but I had heard other people talking about it from time to time. There were rides, games, food, and I was told everything about the whole place almost exploded with fun. In other words, it didn't sound like something that my father would plan on purpose without having an evil plan of his own in mind.

Maybe I would wake up to find that my whole life had just been one long, crazy nightmare. That's what it seemed like. The things that had happened seemed so crazy and farfetched that I had a hard time believing a lot of it myself. If I found it all too nuts to be true, no one else would ever believe me even if I did come up with the courage to tell them.

Breaking through my thoughts I heard Caroline. She sounded as if she would just jump right out of her skin with excitement, "Emily, didn't you hear me? The State Fair... we might go I said!" She was standing right next to my chair as if to make sure that I could actually hear her this time around.

"I heard you. I'm just not sure if I would want to go or not," I said matter of factually.

"What?! How could you not want...," Mom came back up from the cellar and into the kitchen just then, which made Caroline stop talking for the time being.

I wanted so badly to begin asking my mother all kinds of questions right then. But I knew that I should at least wait until I had put the box of photographs and at least one newspaper clipping safely back where I had taken it from before doing such a thing. So instead of asking her something like, "How did you and Dad meet," I asked, "What do you want me to work on cleaning first?"

"Well, we are going to have every inch of this house thoroughly cleaned by the time we are all done. Hmm, let's have you start upstairs in the boys' room. I want you to strip the beds and bring the bedding down cellar to be washed. Eric's clothes and things need to be cleaned out of there too," she paused after she said that last bit, cleared her throat, and then continued on, "There's no point in keeping that stuff any longer. We can set up a table next to the

Produce Stand to sell some of it. Maybe label it $0.01 each or $0.25 a bag. May as well get what money we can out of the stuff."

I really disliked the idea of this job. I couldn't believe she expected me to be the one to clean his stuff out of the room. It felt like she was asking me to erase Eric from our lives completely. I wondered if she even had any pictures of him or any of us kids besides the few that hung on our living room wall. All I had seen in the few pictures I glanced at were strangers I had never met and never heard of.

"I also want the cobwebs dusted from the ceiling and walls in there and the walls washed down. Dust anything that can be dusted. Wash the window and then sweep and mop the floor. That should all keep you busy for a while. Caroline, you're going to do the same in your room. Then you two can come find me. It will probably be time for lunch or later by then."

First I went to bring our card table out next to the Produce Stand. It would be easier to arrange Eric's clothes if the table was already in place for me.

I had so many things on my mind. There was so much that I didn't know which thing to focus my thoughts on first. There was the question of what Dad and Johnny were doing now and where they were. There was the fact that I had just found out that my parents were actually brother and sister. There was so much. A mother and her daughter had been kidnapped and murdered by my father with the help of Johnny and me. Then my father had murdered a police officer in our barn. Caroline had also told me that our father had killed her friend and her friend's mother. Now there was this newest idea of going to the State Fair. There was also my newly found information that my only set of grandparents and my aunt had been murdered. I was beginning to get a headache and I didn't think that I had made it even halfway through the long list of things that were haunting my mind at the moment.

I dug the card table out of where it had been stored in the shed. It was full of dust, dirt, and bugs. I would have to go back into the house to grab a rag to scrub it down with. I hurried into the house, not wanting to spend too long on just setting the table up. Johnny's room would take me long enough to clean. My mother had still called it, "the boys' room". I supposed maybe after I had Eric's stuff cleaned out of there it would officially be just Johnny's room.

I entered the kitchen through the screen door. Caroline was there at the sink, filling a bucket with water. "Where's Mom," I asked, thinking that maybe I could replace the box if she was busy enough with something.

"Didn't you see her outside? She said she was going to gather vegetables for tonight's dinner." The bucket was now half full and Caroline turned off the faucet.

"I can help you with that if you can wait a couple of minutes," I said. I could have her keep watch again and do that coughing thing she did before if Mom happened to come back in.

"Oh thank you Emily!" I explained that I needed her to do as she had done before for me. She began to refuse, but I told her if she did that I would get Mom to let me tell her a story before bed tonight. That was all it took to convince her.

I got the box from its hiding place in my poor excuse for a room. I then delivered it safely without any problems to its original resting spot in Mom and Dad's bedroom closet. Whew, now I would have at least one last thing to worry about.

Mom came in from outside just as I was entering the kitchen again. I began to carry the bucket of soapy water to Caroline's room as I had told her I would. Mom had asked why I was carrying it for her and I explained to her that it would be easier to carry the bucket for Caroline than to have to clean up all the spills she would be sure to make on the way if she had done it herself. She nodded in understanding.

On the way back downstairs from Caroline's room, my mind started to wander back to my list of worries. The current biggest worry I had was Johnny. With the way Dad had been, especially lately, he and Johnny could be almost anywhere doing just about anything imaginable and even something unimaginable was not out of the question. As much as I feared my father, I hoped for Johnny's sake that they returned home soon.

Mom was at the table when I walked into the kitchen again. She quickly stopped the drink she had been taking from her bottle and slipped it back into her apron pocket. I pretended not to notice. I really didn't care anymore whether she drank or not.

Remembering that I had originally gone into the house for a wash rag, I grabbed one from the stack under the kitchen sink. I thought about the fact that Mom and Dad were brother and sister as I grabbed a little pail to put soapy water in. Now that the box of pictures was back in its place I could bring up the subject with her. I began running the water into the pail and asked my mother as conversationally as I could, "Mom, how did you and Dad meet? I've never heard that story."

She chuckled and put down the knife that she had been peeling potatoes with (she seemed to do that a lot because of me). I searched her face for similarities that she and Dad might share that I hadn't noticed before while she said, "That's a long story Emily and best saved for when we don't have so much work to get done. Now go about what you were doing. I have to grab the clothes and hang them out to dry before it decides to rain."

Of course she didn't have time to explain right then how Dad and she met when she was born and that they had slept across the short hallway from each other for their whole childhood. I'd have to remember to check my parents out for shared family traits when they were both in front of me sometime. I couldn't spot anything immediately that screamed related between the two to me in such a short period of time.

It was quite a beautiful day outside, not too hot and not too cold. It was too bad that I didn't have more work to do out here today. I took my time cleaning the card table even though just a

151

quick wipe would have been good enough.

While I cleaned the table my thoughts traveled off to all of my father's most recent murder victims. The one that bothered me the most to think about was that of the adorable little toddler. I really hoped that she hadn't suffered long. I knew that her flesh had been in the stew we had eaten for dinner and maybe some had even been mixed with our sausage. I tried to think of it as if now she would always be a part of me; like some of her spirit was in the stew that I had eaten and so now it would stay in me. I knew it was a strange thought, but that's how I got past the idea of eating her body without throwing up each time I thought about it. Thankfully I found that people (well, toddlers at least) actually tasted pretty decent, almost like pork. Maybe I was as twisted as I thought my father was.

The table was as clean as it could possibly be now. It was time to go get started cleaning up in the bedroom. Maybe I was stalling because I really didn't want to clean Eric's stuff out of the room. I wanted his things to stay as they were and for him to return to use it all again. I knew that was never going to happen because his dead body was buried in our backyard.

I thought that my father had probably held in his craziness to a certain point but then after he had killed Eric he couldn't do it any longer. That was my thinking anyhow.

I gathered what used to be my little brother's clothes together from the bottom two drawers of the dresser in Johnny's room and carried them out to the table I had set up near the road. I laid them all out carefully: pants in one pile, shirts in another. Most of them had been Johnny's before they were Eric's. I taped the sign I had made while in the house the last time to front of the table. If it rained I would probably have to make a new one. I hoped if another little boy wore any of these clothes, he would do happier things in them than Eric had been able to.

I worked a long time in that room to get everything that my mother had told me to do finished. The whole time I thought about Eric and Johnny too. Dad and Johnny weren't back even by the time

I had finished.

My mother had been wrong about me finishing in time for lunch. It had to be well past noon and probably close to dinner time by the time I was finally done. My stomach was growling to let me know I was starving as I carried the bucket of filthy water back down the stairs. It didn't help that I could smell something delicious that made my mouth water. I thought I could smell cooked onions and potatoes and something else.

"Are you finished up there yet," Mom asked, sounding annoyed that it had taken me so long.

"Yes, all done. I just have to dump this bucket now." I carried the bucket towards the screen door so I could dump it outside in the grass.

"Okay, then get back in here and clean yourself up before supper. We didn't get half as much done today as I wanted. We'll have to continue the rest of it tomorrow."

I dumped the bucket of almost black water out off to the side of the house where no one would be likely to step anytime soon. Then I went back in to wash up a bit. I couldn't help but think to myself, "Who cares if the house is clean? No one else ever sees it anyhow and even if they do, Dad makes sure that they don't live for long afterwards."

My plate was already fixed and sitting at my spot on the table. It looked delicious. We were having escalloped potatoes and ham and my mother always put a lot of ham in when she made it. Mom and Caroline were already seated and eating their own food. I joined them and didn't waste any time starting in on my own plate. I loved the creaminess and the taste of the potatoes, ham, and onion all mixed together. I had helped Mom make this before so I knew what was in it.

The three of us were all through eating and I had already started washing the dishes when Dad and Johnny arrived. They both looked exhausted. I didn't feel bad for Dad at all. He brought whatever came to him completely on himself. Johnny, on the other hand, was just one more innocent victim of Dad.

They sat down at the table while Mom made their plates for them. Johnny looked as if he could fall asleep right where he sat. I wondered what they had done during all the time that they were gone. Then I thought about it a little more and realized that I probably didn't really want to know.

Neither my father nor Johnny spoke while they ate. I had finished with the rest of the dishes and had to wait until they were finished to wash theirs as well. I sat back down at the table to wait patiently.

Now I could take a couple of minutes to search for similarities in my parents' looks. I scanned each of their faces, trying not to get caught looking at each of them for so long. The only thing that I could easily point out was that they both had blue eyes, but even those were different shades of blue.

Well, maybe they weren't actually brother and sister after all, I thought hopefully. Maybe one of them had been adopted or was a foster child or something. But the newspaper hadn't said that. I would have to go through the box some other time to find the picture of my grandparents and see if that would answer any of my questions. I knew my parents would never tell me the truth.

Finally, they were done with their plates. Johnny went upstairs to his room and Dad and Mom went out to the living room. I washed the last couple of dishes, dried, and put them away and then I went down to my own room in the cellar.

My brain was exhausted. I needed an off switch for all of my thoughts. The voice I had heard the other night came back then. "I can help you if you'd just let me. Then you could rest."

I looked around. No one was down here with me. I looked over at Julie and saw that she was lying where I had left her, right on my pillow. I tried to cover my ears so that I wouldn't be able to hear the voice. She spoke again anyways, "That won't work and you know it. Let me help you Emily."

I was starting to freak out. Feeling scared and alone, I whispered with my ears still covered by my hands, "No! Please just leave me alone! I don't want to be crazy!"

The voice didn't speak again that night. I fell asleep without even writing in my journal. Julie haunted my dreams. I woke twice screaming and dripping with sweat. I knew if I let her have her way that it would mean I had given up control of my mind. I couldn't let that happen.

Yes, she had always been the little voice in my head that spoke to me, but never as if she were a whole different person than me. I really had thought that maybe she was just my conscious. Now I knew different and it scared the crap out of me.

I didn't mean to scare Emily. I didn't want her to be afraid of me and I didn't want to cause her more upset or worry. I was sure that soon she would be ready for my help, but I guess she wasn't quite there yet.

I felt relieved that she put that stupid box of pictures back where she found it. At least now she wouldn't get caught with it. Plus, I didn't think that she needed to be adding more worries to herself right now with everything else that she had to think and worry about.

The idea of her father suggesting they go to the State Fair was just scary. Of course he wouldn't do something like that without having something horrible in mind to do while they were there. I couldn't think of what he might possibly want to go there for with the whole family, but I was sure that it was something especially rotten and evil. Hopefully they wouldn't end up going after all.

CHAPTER TWENTY-SEVEN

No more was said the next day about the possibility of us going to the State Fair. Maybe Caroline had just gotten overly excited about a wish that my mother had accidentally said out loud. Or maybe Dad had changed his mind about taking all of us. Whatever the case might be, I was fine with it.

According to what my mother had said yesterday, we would be busy cleaning house all day long again today. That was fine with me too. I had already finished washing the breakfast dishes and had started cleaning in the bathroom. Mom wanted me to paint the trim in the bathroom green. I didn't think it was a good color choice, but it wasn't my decision to make. It didn't really matter much what color the trim was anyways. Mom was teaching Caroline how to do her own wash and while the clothes were washing Caroline was working on dusting the living room. Mom was washing all the windows in the house while Caroline dusted. Dad and Johnny were both working outdoors.

While I scrubbed the forever stained porcelain tub I thought. I thought about my murdered grandparents. What had they been like? Did my grandfather do the same terrible things to his children (two of them being my mother and father most likely) that Dad did to us?

Why were they killed? And were they actually my father's very first victims along with my aunt? Why was she killed? My head was beginning to hurt and the tub was as clean as it was going to get.

I moved on to cleaning the nasty toilet. It would never look clean no matter how much I scrubbed. Who was the other couple I had seen in my nightmare? Were they relatives of ours as well? Maybe they were no one and my imagination had made them up. I should have kept the box of pictures longer until I had found pictures of my grandparents and of the other couple I had seen. But I had been too afraid of being caught with the box in with my stuff.

When I was done cleaning and painting the trim in the bathroom my mother took the paintbrush from me so she could soak it in turpentine to get clean. Then she really shocked me and told me to start carrying my stuff back up to my old bedroom, the one I had shared with Caroline. I was confused, happy, excited, scared, and disappointed all at the same time.

The first thing that I thought of was the journals I had started to keep since moving into the cellar. I could not bring them upstairs with me because they would surely be discovered and read. What would I do with them? Would they be safe if I left them right where they were hidden in the wall behind the loose brick? Leaving them where they were already well hidden would probably be my safest choice considering there really were no others. I wouldn't get very many chances, if any at all, to write any more in my newest journal or to stash money away.

The second thing on my mind was the question of why my parents suddenly wanted to allow me to move out of the cellar and back to my old bedroom upstairs. They had moved me down there to separate my sister and me in the first place. I had thought at the time that it was to separate us anyhow. My parents had not wanted me influencing my sister to act out the way that I had been doing. They also wanted to punish me for supposedly lying about the things I said my father had been doing to us kids. That's what I had been led to believe. Plus with my sister and I being in separate parts of the house it was easier for my father to pay either one of us a private visit.

It suddenly dawned on me that maybe there was more to all of this house cleaning and room switching than I realized. Maybe my parents were expecting a visit from someone and trying to make a good first impression. Or maybe they didn't know when the next person would come snooping around and my father didn't think it would be a good idea to have to kill him or her.

It would be a good thing to be back upstairs in the bedroom that I had shared with my little sister. We would be able to talk again the way that we used to and I would be able to comfort her when she needed it. Just sleeping in the same room with her again would be a huge comfort to me. Maybe I would also now be able to stop imagining that my doll was talking to me. I hoped so. I was really beginning to scare myself with that.

I realized as I was lugging my nightstand up the stairs that I had returned my mother's box of pictures just in time. Thank God for small favors. I'm not sure what might have happened if I had been caught with that but I know that it wouldn't have been good. At least I didn't have to worry about that.

Caroline almost knocked me over when she realized what I was doing. She seemed more happy and excited than I was about it. I was surprised that she had not already heard the plan for me to move back in with her. After all of the excitement was out of the way, my mother urged Caroline to get back to work on cleaning the living room.

Johnny was sent in from outside to help me carry my bed back up to my old room. The bed was really heavy and I wasn't very much help for poor Johnny. We both struggled up the stairs because of my lack in strength and height. I apologized as I stopped to lean against the wall.

As soon as we were still he seemed to check around for anyone that might be listening. When it looked as if he was sure there was no one he said, "Find a reason for you and Caroline not to go to The

Fair. Get the stomach bug or something. Whatever you have to do, you two cannot go. Dad's planning on taking all of us the day after tomorrow. So tomorrow night before bed you should start to fake some symptoms. You know this is important Emily, or I wouldn't tell you to do this."

"Why Johnny? And what about you?" The door to the cellar opened just as I finished asking the last question and, of course, it was our father. He seemed to be able to somehow sense when he was least wanted and always seemed to show up at that time. Of course, as far as I knew he was never really wanted around by any of us children.

"I thought Johnny might need a stronger hand with that bed than yours. Move out of the way Emily. Go help your mother with dinner or something." He grabbed my shoulders and almost pushed me past him up the stairs.

How was I ever going to talk Caroline into pretending that she was sick so she wouldn't be able to go to The Fair? She was so excited about the idea of going. I knew if Johnny was warning me to do whatever I had to do to stay home that he knew that Dad had something truly wicked planned for that day. Would our father even accept Caroline and me both being sick as an excuse for staying home? Or would he force us to tag along either way, sick or not?

I had to think about this and plan it well. It sounded like it was very important that I got this right and didn't screw it up. Maybe I should really make us both sick somehow, or at least Caroline, so that it was more believable and I didn't have to convince her to fake it.

Then Julie spoke to me again. "I have a great idea to help you." I didn't fight the voice or stop her, but instead listened closely to all that she had to say. I would have to wait until just before dinner tomorrow to carry out her plan though. It would work to keep Caroline and me away from the Fair, I was sure of that. I wished that I could find a way to keep Johnny home too, but I knew the plan wouldn't work for him. I wondered what Johnny knew. What could my father possibly have planned now?

My mother was outside gathering eggs. "Do you need any help with dinner tonight?"

"Maybe. I thought I would make a broccoli and cheese quiche, French toast, bacon, and sausage. We haven't had breakfast for supper in a long time. You can go in and start frying up the bacon if you will."

Mom was inside and already preparing the quiche by the time I started to actually fry the bacon. She started talking more to herself than to me it seemed, "Tomorrow night we're having pinto beans for supper so we'll have to start soaking the beans tonight."

When I heard that I was glad that tomorrow night Caroline and I probably wouldn't be able to eat dinner because we would be too ill. I hated pinto beans and Dad always made us sit at the table until our bowls were completely empty. There was usually crying involved on pinto bean nights, not by me anymore, but because of Caroline and Eric. Now there was only Caroline left to cry.

Dad and Johnny both came bounding down the stairs and into the kitchen. Dad spoke to me, "Okay, your bed's all set. Now you just have to get everything situated. Go do it now. Your mom can finish making dinner on her own." Wow, there had to be another reason behind getting the house in shape and moving my bedroom back to its original place, especially if my father was going to let me skip out in the middle of helping Mom fix dinner.

I was so pleased to have all of my things back in my old, familiar bedroom. For now I was alone in here. Caroline was still downstairs cleaning the living room spotless. I felt almost as if I was skipping out on everyone by being up here just sorting my things. But Johnny and Caroline both knew that I was only doing as I was told and would get punished if I didn't listen.

My mind wandered, as it had a tendency to do when I worked. I wondered if this was the room that my mother shared with her little sister years ago or if this had been my father's room. At some point I would ask one or both of my parents these questions. I just had to pick the perfect time to do it.

My stuff was all back in its proper places finally. It didn't take that long at all once I got started. My clothes were all back in my drawers in the dresser, I had put clean sheets on my bed and a clean pillowcase on my pillow, Julie was tucked neatly under my blanket on top of my pillow, and my story writing stuff was back in my nightstand. I took my dirty sheets down to the washer and threw them in, hardly believing that I had slept down in this dark, musty place just last night.

It was time for dinner when I had finished everything I needed to do to get my room in order. I loved French toast with sausage. I didn't care much for the quiche, but I had to take at least a small piece. It was one of Dad's many rules.

Our father talked excitedly while he ate about taking us all to the State Fair on Friday, the day after tomorrow. Caroline screeched for joy at the mention of it. I knew I had better pretend to be thrilled as well so I said, "That sounds like fun. I've always wanted to go to the Fair."

Dad was still really worked up about it and said through a mouthful of food, "It will certainly be a day none of you will ever forget, I'm sure!" With that statement I had no doubt in my head at all that I would need to do as Johnny had said and make sure that Caroline and I would not be able to attend Dad's joyous event. Julie's idea should work perfectly to make sure that we were both too ill to be able to go.

Once dinner was over and Caroline had helped me wash, dry, and put away the dishes we went up to our room. Happy tears formed in the corners of my eyes at the thought of not having to sleep down in the cellar all by myself again. Caroline asked me to tell her one of my stories and that's when I couldn't help it any longer and the tears began to fall.

"I'm sorry Emily. You don't have to tell me a story if you don't want to."

I laughed while still sobbing and then said as I wiped the tears from my face, "No, I will. I'm just so happy to be sharing a bedroom with you again. I've missed you Caroline."

I told her a story after we both already had our pajamas on for the night. Then I told her that tomorrow we would have a tea party sometime before dinner, just her and I. We would have some girl time together and use the heirloom tea set Mom had given me for my eleventh birthday. She was thrilled.

I slept more comfortably that night than I had since leaving this room and my little sister about a month or so beforehand. My bed was still the same and still smelled a little bit like the cellar, but it was having Caroline so close to me that made me feel so much better. I wondered what her time alone in this room had been like. Hopefully it hadn't been as bad as my time all the way downstairs.

Nobody bothered either one of us all night. I woke the next morning feeling well rested and pretty good. Then we did the normal everyday summer things like getting dressed, making our beds, eating breakfast, washing the dishes, and helping Mom tidy up the house before lunch. We would be starting our school lessons again right after the State Fair was over. That was when we always started for the year.

Emily was finally starting to listen to me even though she realized that I wasn't really her conscious after all. I was so happy and relieved. She needed my idea to help her get out of going to the Fair and I was sure nothing less would work. That man must have something really terrible planned for Emily's brother to warn her to fake sick or whatever she had to do to stay home. I was curious what he had up his sleeve, but I was thankful that Emily was finally going to listen to me and not have to find out. Hopefully she would go through with the plan. If not, I would have to try to take over to make sure that she did.

CHAPTER TWENTY-EIGHT

After we all had lunch and the dishes had been washed I asked Mom if Caroline and I could play for just a short while. She agreed but told me we only had about half an hour and then we needed to get back to helping with the chores. I thanked her and then ran outside, grabbing the cup that she had used to soak the paintbrush I had used in. I left the paintbrush on the sill of the window outside. Then I walked back into the house and upstairs to my bedroom, being careful not to be seen with the cup.

The turpentine dirtied with green paint looked just like tea to me, just like Julie had said it did. Good enough to play pretend with my little sister and make us both convincingly sick. I got out my antique tea set, being careful not to bang any of the pieces together too hard. I poured only a little of the turpentine into the tea pot. I wanted to make us both sick, not kill us.

Once I had everything all arranged neatly on the throw rug in our room I called to Caroline. "Caroline, come have a tea party with me!"

Only a few seconds had passed before I could hear her running up the stairs to our bedroom. We both sat on the floor in front of our tea cups. "Would you care for some tea, madam," I asked in the best rich person voice that I could come up with.

Caroline giggled and then answered in her funny talk, "Yes please, that would be simply lovely."

I felt like such a horrible sister for what I was about to do to Caroline. I knew in my head that I was doing it for her own good. Also I tried to keep in mind that she wouldn't have to suffer alone since I would be drinking the poison right along with her. I forced a smile and then poured us both some of the stuff from the tea pot.

"Cheers," I said, picking my cup up while holding my pinky out like the proper ladies from my books always did while drinking tea. Caroline followed my example.

I realized almost immediately after I took my sip that this whole idea of Julie's was probably a terrible mistake. Either that or Julie was really just trying to kill us. Caroline and I both started coughing. It felt like my lips, tongue, and throat were burning and my stomach started hurting worse than I ever remembered it hurting in my life. I began heaving and throwing up right on the bare floor of my bedroom. Caroline was puking now too.

I wanted to comfort my little sister but I couldn't. I was in too much pain and couldn't stop throwing up myself. I was trying to decide whether I should go for help or not when I was able. I didn't know whether this was something that we could die from or not and with the way I was feeling I was really scared that it might be. Then I thought, "Oh well, Julie would be doing us both a favor if we did end up dying. Our suffering would be over once and for all." I decided not to tell anyone what I had done. Hopefully this would at least keep Caroline and I home from The Fair tomorrow.

When I could I made my way down to the kitchen to get Caroline and I both some water to help wash away the turpentine from our mouths and throats. I was pretty sure none of it could be left in our stomachs. Thankfully no one was around to see the condition I was in at that time. I brought the water back upstairs and told Caroline to drink.

My throat felt like it was on fire, but I needed to give Caroline some important instructions. "Are you okay Caroline?"

"I think so. My throat and tummy still hurt though."

"Good. Now listen to me carefully."

I looked away to cough again. Then I continued, "We are going to tell Mom that we don't feel good and that we are throwing up. She'll be able to look at us and see that we're sick. Don't tell her it was from drinking the tea or I will be in dead trouble. Do you hear me?"

Poor Caroline looked so confused. She was still coughing but managed to reply to me, "Did you make us sick on purpose Emily? Why did you do that?"

I felt terrible. What a mean sister I was to do something like that to her. I knew in my head I had done the right thing. I just wish I didn't have to feel so rotten about doing it.

"Listen Caroline. I'm sorry I made us sick. I really am. Johnny told me I had to so we wouldn't have to go to The Fair tomorrow. He told me that something really awful is going to happen there and we had to find a way to stay home. Please promise not to tell on me and act like you're sicker than you are so we can stay home. Please? I know you really wanted to go, but it's not going to be the fun time that you want."

"Emily…," she whined. Then she stopped and looked like she was thinking hard about what I had said. "What's going to happen at The Fair that's so bad that we can't go?"

"I don't know Caroline. All I know is that if Johnny begged me to do whatever I had to in order for you and I to both be able to stay home it must be more awful than anything we could imagine. Please do what I asked you to and just trust me."

"Okay Caroline."

Her chin quivered and she started crying. I knew she wanted to go tomorrow more than anything and that it broke her heart hearing that we had to stay home. It broke my heart to have to be the one to make her so sick in the first place and then to have to tell her the news that she wouldn't be able to go to The Fair that she had been so excited about.

I held Caroline in my arms and let her cry. When she was finally through I cleaned up my tea set and put it back in my hope chest in the corner of our room. Then I cleaned up the vomit from the floor. I had to roll up the throw rug and carry it downstairs to scrub and hang outside. I told Caroline to lie down in her bed to rest. I let her know that I would deal with telling our mother that we had the stomach bug or something. She unhappily agreed and climbed into her bed as I left the room.

Mom was in the kitchen now pulling freshly baked bread out of the oven. "Mom, I don't feel too good. Caroline and I just got sick all over on our floor. I have to clean our rug still. Is it okay if we both skip dinner tonight and just go to bed early?"

"You look terrible Emily! Is Caroline okay or should I go up and check on her?"

"I think she'll be alright. I think it might be a stomach bug or something. She's laying down now and that's what I'm going to do when I'm done cleaning the rug."

"Oh geez. Hopefully you both are better by morning so you can go to The Fair. Don't worry about the rug. I'll clean it. You go get rested up so you can get better."

"Thanks Mom. I hope we can go too. Caroline's so sad

thinking that she won't be able to go." I grabbed another glass of water to take up to our room.

I changed into my nightgown and then drank half of the water in the glass. It felt wonderful on my sore mouth and throat. I offered the other half of the water to my sister. She drank it down as if she were in the middle of a desert and hadn't had anything to drink in days.

I woke some time later in the night to the not uncommon sounds of my parents yelling at each other. I crept out of bed as quietly as I could and went to listen by my door. I heard only bits and pieces of what my mother said, "Why - - - fake – sick?" They must be arguing about Caroline and me possibly not being able to go to The Fair.

Then my father I could hear more clearly, "I don't know. You're right, they probably wouldn't. We'll see how they are tomorrow." He still yelled what he had said, even though he was admitting to being wrong. Realizing that my mother was right and he was not must have made him even more upset.

I really hoped that Mom would still go with Dad to The Fair. I didn't want Johnny to go if something terrible was going to take place, but I wouldn't mind having both of my parents out of the house so that I could look through that box of pictures more.

My curiosity was really beginning to get the better of me since the quick look I had taken before. That had only created more questions, but it answered questions that I never realized I had before as well. Besides, I deserved to know what my background was. I would find out early enough tomorrow if I'd be able to do some more looking. I fell asleep wondering what else I might find in my mother's mysterious box of memories.

Why did Emily always try to go from one bad thing to the next? Why couldn't she just take the day off and relax without creating any more worries with her little sister? Going through that box of her mother's was not a good idea, not in my opinion at least.

At least the turpentine thing had worked how I had hoped that it would. I had actually gotten the idea from Emily's father. I heard him talking to her mother one day about a news story he read. A young girl and her brother had both been admitted to the hospital after drinking turpentine while having a tea party. The story stuck in my head and I was glad because it came in very handy today. I never did find out what happened to the girl and her brother after that though. I guess it was a good thing that Emily and her sister didn't seem deathly ill at least.

CHAPTER TWENTY-NINE

The next day I woke to hear a hustle and bustle from downstairs that I was not used to. I hurried to shake Caroline from her sleep. "How are you feeling this morning?"

"Tired and my throat still hurts." She leaned up on her left elbow and looked at me.

"Mom or Dad will be up here any minute to check on us. Try to make yourself puke over the side of your bed or something. I'll clean it." I was sitting up on the edge of my bed.

"How am I s'posed to do that?" She looked disgusted at what I had suggested.

"Stick your fingers down your throat. Try to touch that punching bag thingy in the back." I did it myself to show her what I meant, immediately making myself get sick all over my own lap and the floor.

"Eew Emily!"

"Just do it,"

I whispered as loudly and angrily as I could at her while I shook the slimy vomit from my fingers onto the floor. She did as I ordered and successfully vomited all over the side of her bed. Perfect, I was positive we would have no problems at all being allowed to stay home today.

"Stay in bed. I'll start cleaning this mess up." I stood up and carefully dodged the vomit that was covering the floor between our two beds.

Mom greeted me in the kitchen, "How are you two feeling today? Is Caroline awake yet?" She was packing up what looked like lunches to take to The Fair.

"She's awake but we're both still puking. I have a mess to clean on our floor." I bent down to look for something from under the sink to help clean the mess. A bucket with soapy water would have to do.

"Ugh Emily, there's some on the front of your nightgown too. Well, I guess you two will have to stay home today. Do you think you can take care of the both of you if we leave you here alone?"

Yes! That's what I had been hoping to hear. I didn't dare ask if Johnny could stay to help take care of us because that might make her think that she should stay home instead. I wanted to look through that box again so badly that it made my mouth water, which was weird.

Trying to sound unhappy about not being able to join them at The Fair I replied, "I think so. We'll probably just stay in bed all day anyways. I don't feel very well." I ran the water in the sink until it became hot, added some dish soap to the bottom of the bucket, and then filled the bucket with the hot water. I made sure to grab a couple of rags as well. Then I headed upstairs to start cleaning the mess that I had created.

Dad ended up coming up to our room, I guess to make sure that we really were sick like I had said. He opened the door as I was scraping up a pile of puke from the floor with one of the rags. He brought his shirt up over his nose when he realized what I was doing and then asked, "Are you sure you girls will be alright here on your own today? I can have your mother stay with you if you think you might need her." How thoughtful of him.

"We'll be fine Dad," I replied while rinsing my rag in the hot, soapy water. Then to make him feel better about it I added, "We'll probably both stay in bed all day anyways with the way we're both feeling." I wondered what he had planned for today. Maybe Johnny would tell me some other time.

With his shirt still over his nose our father said, "Okay. Well, we're gonna hit the road here in a few minutes I think. Don't answer the door to nobody. I hope you two get to feeling better quick." He left, shutting our door behind him.

Yes, yes, yes! I was so excited for Caroline and me to have the house all to ourselves for probably the entire day. I would have plenty of time to look through Mom's entire box of pictures and figure out who was who. Maybe I would even write in my journal when I went down to the cellar to throw Caroline's bedding in the washer. Other than worrying about Johnny, I thought that today would be a pretty great day.

Mom came to our room to check on Caroline and I one last time before leaving for the day. Caroline was lying down in her bed and doing a great job of being sick. I had just finished cleaning the puke from the floor and was about to tell my sister to get up so I could strip her bed when our mother came in. Mom kissed each of us on the forehead and said that they would be leaving as soon as she got back downstairs. All of this concern over us girls being sick was almost too much to handle.

I had a feeling that Emily was going to screw everything up by trying to look through that stupid box of old pictures. I was sure that she would get caught. Or if she didn't get caught, she would find out something that would make her feel even worse about everything and make her worry more than she already did.

I also hoped that whatever Emily's father had planned for the Fair somehow didn't happen. Emily didn't need to hear about any other bad stuff that her father did and she didn't need something happening to her older brother either. She didn't need to have to deal with any more kidnapped people either if that's what he was going to try to do. Hopefully nothing would happen or at least hopefully Emily would never find out what it was that happened.

CHAPTER THIRTY

I listened as hard as I could for the engine of the truck to start and then to leave the driveway. I couldn't wait to get started with the rest of my day. I promised Caroline I would tell her a lot of stories throughout the day and baby her like crazy when I wasn't busy. This made her slightly happier about having to stay home instead of going with the rest of our family to The Great New York State Fair.

I stripped Caroline's bed and told her I would make it up with clean bedding when I came back up from downstairs. I told her to go get a bowl of cereal to eat or some toast or something if she was hungry. She could do either of those things on her own without any help from me.

Then I rethought my plans. "Never mind. I'll make us both a little something to eat and bring it right up here for you." I didn't want to write in my diary until after I took a look through Mom's box again. I would throw Caroline's blankets in the wash, make us both a light breakfast, put the clean bedding on her bed, and then I would go downstairs into my parents' bedroom to look through that box of pictures. Then I would check on Caroline again before going down to write in my journal. After all that, Caroline's blankets should be done in the wash and I could hang them out to dry. Then I would spend the rest of the day taking care of my little sister as I had promised that I would.

I carried my sister's puked bedding down to the washer. It was hard to believe when I went down in that gloomy, musty place that I had actually slept down here every night for a while until last night. I threw the blankets in the washer, added some soap, and then headed back upstairs to make me and my sister a little something to eat.

I decided some whole wheat toast and orange juice would be the best thing on our stomachs after my stunt with the "tea". We needed to eat something to help get that nasty stuff out of our bodies. I could still feel several of its effects on my own body, so I knew that Caroline must still have some too. I made our food and brought it right up to our room for us to enjoy.

The orange juice stung my sore mouth and throat. Maybe orange juice wasn't the best choice after all. I knew that it was healthy and should help clean that poison out of our bodies though. We both finished all of our toast and juice. Caroline looked worn out to me.

"I'll put that clean bedding on your bed for you now. Then you should lie down for a while. You look beat. I'll read you a quick story before I take our plates downstairs." I began to head towards our door to go to the hall closet for the bedding.

"Thank you Emily." She was sitting on my bed, barely able to keep herself upright.

"You can go ahead and lie down on my bed for a minute until I'm done if you want."

I was so eager to get to that box and see what else I might find in there that it was hard to think about anything else. I managed to focus long enough to grab a clean pillowcase, clean bottom sheet and top sheet, and the only clean bedspread as quickly as I could. Then I went back into our room and made Caroline's bed faster than I think I had ever made a bed up before in my whole life. She was already asleep on my bed. I decided to let her be and happily almost ran down the stairs to get my hands on Mom's secret box of pictures.

Julie tried talking to me again. I tried to ignore her voice and act like I couldn't hear her, but I did. She was telling me that she thought looking through the pictures was a bad idea. I didn't care. I was going to do it anyways whether she liked it or not.

Grrr! That stubborn little girl won't listen to me. I know she hears me so for her to pretend that she doesn't is just stupid. I just hope she doesn't get caught. If she finds more stuff to worry about because of something she might find in the box, I'll just have to deal with that later. She could really use a nap instead, but again, she won't listen to me. She might need her rest, she had no idea what her father might be up to at The Fair or whether she would be able to sleep after they got home.

CHAPTER THIRTY-ONE

As I was digging the box back out of my parents' closet, I wondered whether I should bring the box up to my room or just look through it right where I was. I wasn't sure whether I would be able to hear the truck from either bedroom if it pulled into the driveway and that would be extremely important. I decided to bring the box into the living room with me. I would be able to hear any vehicle that might pull in from there and could put the box back where I had gotten it from with time enough not to get caught.

For some reason I was really nervous about looking through the box again. Actually, it was probably for several different reasons: 1) I was scared to death of being caught with my mother's box; 2) I was terrified of what more I might find out about my family that I was better off not knowing; and 3) I wasn't sure what I should actually do with any information that I did happen to find.

I walked through the hall and into the living room. I sat myself on the edge of the couch and set the box on the coffee table. I opened the curtains behind the couch so that I would be able to see better. If they happened to come home and found the curtains open,

I could just say that I saw that they were closed and opened them like we did every other day so that no one would think that we were all gone or something.

"Well, we deserve to know and I'm going to find out all I can," I heard myself say out loud (and it was actually me speaking, not Julie) as I lifted the lid off the old shoe box. I rummaged through a bunch of photos that seemed pretty boring. I could look through those more carefully some other time, if another chance ever came up. If not, it wouldn't be that big of a deal. I needed to look for pictures of the two couples and the little girl that I had seen in my nightmare. Hopefully there would be writing on the backs to tell me who the people were. Maybe there would be more newspaper clippings to read as well.

Then I saw it. The picture of the couple that I thought must be my grandparents fell out of the small stack that I was holding and landed right on my lap. Chills came over me when I realized that the man and woman in the photograph looked just like one of the couples in my nightmare.

I hurried to turn the photograph over and sure enough there was writing there:

Mom and Dad (Henry and Emma Fleischer) - May 1961

My grandfather looked so much older than my grandmother and according to that newspaper article I had read, he was. I wondered what their story was: how they met, if they were in love, what each of them was like, and all of that. Neither one of my grandparents looked very happy at all in this picture. I saw features in both of my grandparents that my mother and father each had. My father looked mostly like my grandfather, but he did have my grandmother's eyes. My mother looked mostly like my grandmother, but she had my grandfather's eyes and it looked like she probably had my grandfather's chunkiness as well.

I set their picture aside and shuffled some more through the pictures until I came to one with three children in it. Two of the children were my mother and father, I could tell. The other must have been my murdered aunt that I had seen in my nightmare, just younger in this picture. I looked at the back of that photo and found this:

Johnny- 8 years old
Ruth- 6 years old
Ann- 10 months old

Ann was the only one smiling in the picture. However, in this picture you could at least tell that they were all definitely brother and sisters more than you could by looking at them now.

I moved on. I wanted to hurry and get through the entire box long before anyone came back home. I still didn't see a photo of the other angry couple that had showed up in my nightmare. Maybe they hadn't been our relatives. Then I found another piece of paper at the very bottom of the box, another newspaper article. The headline was: *Horrific Scene Discovered at Fair.* It read:

"Authorities discovered the bodies of a man and woman at the New York State Fair Friday night. The man appeared to have been beaten to death with some sort of blunt instrument. The coroner believed the woman to be heavily pregnant at the time of the attack. He also believes the infant was removed from the woman's abdomen and the woman subsequently bled out, leading to her death. The infant was not found at the scene and police believe the couple's attacker may still have the baby and that the baby may have been the entire reason behind the attack. Police are seeking any…"

"Oh my God!" I looked for the date of the article and found it: September 3rd, 1922. I quickly did the math in my head. I was good with numbers, just like I seemed to be smart in almost every area. I must have gotten that from my mother because my father didn't seem that smart to me at all. Of course, if they were brother and sister, I actually would have gotten that from both of them, whether my dad was smart or not. I was starting to confuse even myself.

My grandmother would have been born around that time. That infant was probably her. My grandfather was a good twenty years older than my grandmother. He could have easily been the one who killed her parents and took her. What the hell kind of a family did I have?

Part of the paper crumbled in my hand. "Shit," I swore out loud for the first time in my life. I quickly put the paper back in the box, being more careful with it than I had already been so it wouldn't fall apart any more than it already had. I replaced everything else back in the box and then put the lid back on. Good, there were no pieces of paper left anywhere on the couch that I could tell. I took the box back to where it belonged, hidden in my parents' dark closet filled with family secrets.

Thank goodness she at least got that dreadful box put back where it belonged. I had been so afraid that she would get caught with it and then who knew what would happen to her.

I wasn't sure what to think about her newest discovery with the newspaper clipping. I wasn't sure if she was right about the baby in the article being her grandmother or her grandfather being the one to murder her parents and take the baby. I supposed the dates fit, plus why else would her parents or her grandfather keep something like that if it had nothing to do with them? Maybe the murdered couple were relatives of the family somehow and that was why they had kept the article all these years. I wasn't sure. It didn't matter, Emily had made up her mind about the whole thing and now she would think about it nonstop.

CHAPTER THIRTY-TWO

Caroline was still sleeping in my bed where I had left her. I wondered how long ago that had been. Then I saw our plates and cups from breakfast still sitting on my night stand. I couldn't believe I had forgotten to take care of them in my hurry to look through that God awful box. I decided to do that and also check the time.

It was three thirty in the afternoon. The rest of my family could be gone for quite a while yet. I really wondered now what my father's plan was for The Fair. His own father had killed a man and cut a pregnant woman's stomach open to steal her baby during his trip to The Fair.

Well, that was the most likely possibility that I could think of. Why else would that article be hidden in with a box of old photographs of our family? That's probably who the other couple in my nightmare was- my grandmother's parents. I wondered if my grandmother ever saw that article and what she had thought if she did.

So my grandfather was some kind of sick freak too. He was a murderer, a kidnapper, and most likely a guy who liked to do those nasty things to kids just like my own father was. My mother and father were brother and sister. My grandparents were murdered around the time that my mother should have been pregnant for Johnny... I wondered if Johnny was my grandfather's son or my father's. Did my father kill his parents because of what his own father did to them? Or did someone else really come in and kill them like the paper said? It still didn't make sense to me that my father would kill his little sister. Of course, none of this should make sense to any normal person.

The bedding should definitely be done in the washer by now. I decided to get that hung out while there was still plenty of daylight for it to dry by. I grabbed the washed bedding from the washer, threw it in the basket, and carried it out through the door in the kitchen. It was so quiet and peaceful out. If I didn't have so much other crazy stuff on my mind I might actually be able to enjoy the day with some reading or writing. I didn't even feel like writing in my journal anymore. It was all just a little too much. I needed time to think about it all before I wrote any of it down on paper.

I always loved how the wash looked as it was hanging out on the line to dry. It just seemed like such an ordinary housekeeping thing to do and it smelled so nice. Never while hanging laundry did my father or anyone else try to come up to me to do anything yucky, probably because it was outside and in the open.

Washing dishes and other chores inside the house were a completely different story. I couldn't tell you the number of times that my father came up behind me to bring me somewhere to do that horrible thing to me while I was washing dishes or dusting furniture or any of the different other indoor chores. I took one last long whiff of the washed bedding that was hanging and then went back in to the house to check on my sister.

Before I even had the chance to get settled in my room again I heard the front door slam open. Uh oh, they were home and it didn't sound like someone was very happy. "You're just like our father was, aren't you," I heard my mother's angry voice accusing my father. Oh no, this was going to be awful. I wondered what had happened at The Fair and if Johnny was alright. Something wicked must have happened for Mom to slip and say, "Our father," where anyone could have heard her.

Instead of the hitting and furniture throwing that I expected to start hearing I heard Dad say calmly, "What do you want me to say Ruth? What did you expect? I'm sorry. I'll stop, I promise."

I heard footsteps on the stairs and quickly got into my bed. After listening a little more closely I realized that it was my brother's footsteps I was hearing. Thank God he was okay.

Then I heard my mother's voice again, "How will you stop? How long has this been going on and why? You know what it was like when we were little, John!"

My mother sounded like she really didn't know what had been going on under her own nose. Something had happened while they were at The Fair to open up my mother's eyes to the truth of what we had been going through. I wondered if she had gotten the whole picture or just a small part of it.

I heard my father cry. Then I heard both of them walk into the kitchen and then into their bedroom. The door shut behind them and I heard nothing more. No fighting, no muffled voices. I was shocked by what I had just heard. Would things really change now?

I couldn't help myself. I snuck quietly out of my bed and across the hall to Johnny's bedroom.

Johnny turned away from where he had been looking out the window when I came through the door. "Emily what are you doing in here? Do you want to get us both in trouble?"

"What happened at The Fair Johnny?"

"What was supposed to happen or what really happened," he asked in a whisper.

"Both." I sat down on his bed, waiting anxiously to hear what he had to say.

He sighed and then said quietly, "I shouldn't be telling you any of this. You should just be happy you weren't there."

"Please Johnny? I have a bunch of stuff that I found out that I have to tell you too."

"Fine," he sat down next to me and began to tell me all the horrible details of the day, both what was supposed to happen and what had happened instead. Johnny told me that our father had planned to go to The Fair to have his own fun all day with as many little kids as he could. There was going to be some sort of secret sale at one of the tents to sell children for an hour at a time to the highest bidder. Caroline and I were supposed to be in the lineup of available children. I shuddered at the thought of what that might have been like for both Caroline and me.

"Dad also told me to keep my eyes peeled for a wife for myself. He wanted me to just choose any girl at all from The Fair that I may want. Then he was planning for us to just take her. I don't want that. I want someone that actually wants me for who I am.

Anyways, Mom ended up following Dad when she saw that he had one of the little girls from the auction. While she was following him she asked me if what you had told her before was true. I told her it was. She ended up catching him in the act of using the little girl in one of the worker's campers and she seemed horrified. She confronted him right then. I never saw Dad look as ashamed as he did at that moment." Johnny began to get back up from his bed.

I reached my hand over to stop him. "Wait Johnny. There's stuff I have to tell you that I found out."

He sat back down only because I forced him to but seemed like it was hard work having to sit still. "I'll tell you as quick as I can. I saw Mom looking at some pictures one day and crying. When I got the chance I took the box I had seen the pictures in and looked through it. I finished looking through it today while you guys were gone."

"So what," Johnny replied sounding irritated at me. Then he added, "Besides, do you know what could have happened if you got caught snooping in Mom and Dad's bedroom?"

I waved my hands in frustration, "Yes, yes… but listen. I found out a whole bunch of crazy stuff." I went on to tell him everything that I had found in that box. He listened quietly through the whole thing until I was finished.

"Okay. You'd better get back to your room before one of them decides to come up to check on you guys. I need time to think about all of this. Not a word of it to Caroline or anyone. If anyone says anything it will be me."

Emily must have realized somewhere in her mind what Johnny was about to do when he leaned in towards her. She let me take over, finally. He put his lips to Emily's and tried to part them with his tongue. His lips were soft, but his breath smelled like old ketchup and peanut butter. What a disgusting combination that made. I didn't let him get his tongue into her mouth but instead slapped him and said, "Don't you ever try to kiss Emily like that again or you will be sorry."

I found Emily's brother quite attractive myself, but I knew when he looked at me all he saw was his little sister Emily, not me, Julie. So this type of behavior could not be allowed.

He looked shocked and a little confused as he held his cheek and said, "Now go." He almost pushed us out of his bedroom.

Why would he try to kiss Emily like that? I knew that he cared for her, but as an older brother, not as someone who wanted to take advantage of her like her father always did. I was so glad that Emily finally let me take over for her. She didn't need to deal with her brother acting like that on top of everything else. At this point I would have never thought something like that was what it would take for Emily to let me in, but it worked and that was just fine with me. Now the next time would be even easier to take over for her.

CHAPTER THIRTY-THREE

No one checked on Caroline and me for the rest of that evening or even later that night. I guess my parents had been busy with their own much bigger problems. As far as I knew, they didn't leave their bedroom again that day.

Caroline had woken up for a couple of hours and I read a couple of chapters to her from Charlie and the Chocolate Factory as I had promised her I would. We left off at the part where Charlie found the golden ticket. I had read the book before and I knew that she would love it as much as I had.

Then I went downstairs and made the three of us kids a quick dinner of hot dogs and pork and beans. I made sure I saved enough for my mother and father in case they decided that they were hungry later on. Then I brought our suppers upstairs for us to eat so we wouldn't disturb my parents. Johnny chose to eat his dinner alone in his room. While Caroline and I ate she reminded me about the bedding I had left hanging out to dry. I'd have to go bring that in so no spirits could wear the clothes if by chance that story was true.

After Caroline and I were both through eating I took our dishes and Johnny's to the sink. I washed the few dishes that we had dirtied and then dried and put them back in the cupboards. Then I went out to take the bedding off the line and brought the basket back upstairs to fold the sheets and bedspread to put them away in the hall closet.

None of us kids heard any more about The Fair or what had happened there that day. We went on with our lives as we normally would have. Except that my mother seemed to have gotten through to my father's conscience or something of the sort.

His streak of murdering and craziness seemed to finally be over. It had been almost a full month without him trying to do any of the bad stuff to me and I was pretty sure he had left my brother and sister alone in that way as well. He was still very strict with us and still didn't hold back on the beatings of my mother or any of us. At least the other stuff seemed to have come to a stop.

We celebrated Caroline's ninth birthday. For her birthday dinner she chose to have breakfast foods. So for supper that night we had French toast, strawberries, bacon, sausage, scrambled eggs, and orange juice. Then we all sang Happy Birthday to her while she stood smiling in front of her chocolate cake all lit up with candles.

Johnny didn't mention anything to me or anyone else about the things I had told him I found out from snooping through Mom's picture box. I imagined that he was waiting until the right time. Maybe he just wanted to keep those newly found secrets hidden and forget that they were really true. I kept quiet about my findings as well, mostly because I had no idea what to say or who to say it to.

Johnny would soon have a birthday of his own. He was growing up fast and would be leaving us before we knew it to start a new life of his own. Since things had calmed down with my father there was probably no need for him to steal Caroline and me away from our home and our parents.

Life wasn't perfect in the Fleischer household. I didn't expect that it ever would be. I could settle for this new normal that my family seemed to have settled into and be quite satisfied.

I knew that there was always the possibility that the bad things could start happening again. Because of that I never completely let my guard down. That was probably smart on my part.

Not even a month had passed since The Fair. It was a late September night and I heard my father's footsteps as they came up the stairs towards our bedroom. My heart sank into my stomach as our door opened. He told me to take my nightgown off and then he woke Caroline from her sleep. I was terrified of what he could possibly have planned for the two of us. He brought us across the hall to Johnny's bedroom. Apparently this was going to be a family event.

Julie began speaking to me again. I tried like crazy to ignore the voice in my head but as I began to realize what my father wanted us kids to do Julie's voice got stronger. For the second time ever I let her have my mind so that I wouldn't have to really be there for what was taking place. I felt so peaceful; it was like I was sleeping.

Maybe I had just dreamt it all. I woke the next morning and remembered the peaceful drifting into nothing that I had done. However, my girl parts were sore so I knew that it hadn't just been a dream.

My world felt like it had been crushed. I couldn't go back to the way things had been before The Fair. I just couldn't. And I wouldn't accept that I had let myself lose control of my own mind.

After that night life continued as it had after The Fair for about two weeks. Two weeks was a lot longer than my father had waited between those awful visits before The Fair.

I began to worry that something was wrong with me. I began to wake up in the mornings feeling like I needed to puke but nothing really came up. My boobs felt hard as rocks. I wondered if these could still be symptoms of my poisonous tea party. I didn't really believe that since both Caroline and I seemed to have already gotten all better from that tea party long before I started becoming sick every day.

I took a quick bath to clean myself up, got dressed, and then went to eat breakfast with the rest of my family. The whole time I was eating I was wondering whether or not I should tell someone what was going on with me. My thinking was that it probably wouldn't turn out very well right now if I did.

The rest of my family went about their days and I finished my breakfast alone. Dad sent Johnny and Caroline in the truck to town. They were supposed to try to sell some of the last produce left from summer at a lower price than normal. Dad had said that he figured it was worth a try. What they didn't manage to sell through the day we would figure out how to use somehow. Once I was through eating I did what I always did after I ate: the dishes.

After I was finished with the dishes I was supposed to help decorate for Halloween outside. We had a pumpkin patch as usual where people could come to pick out their own pumpkins. This year we would also be hosting a haunted barn that families could pay to walk through and get scared. If people only knew the true horrors that took place there they probably would never come. I would have given anything not to have been a part of it all.

I wished I had been able to go into town with Johnny and Caroline. I really didn't feel like decorating. What I felt like doing was curling up into a ball and sleeping the rest of my childhood away until I was old enough to finally leave this place and its terrible secrets behind.

Emily probably worried as I did that she could be pregnant. I remembered, as she most likely did, how her mother had complained of feeling when she had been pregnant for Eric. The way Emily was feeling sounded an awful lot like that. Poor Emily was only twelve years old, certainly not old enough to be having a baby. She would never be old enough to be having her own father's baby. Maybe I could figure out a way somehow to help her with this problem too.

She didn't know that if she was in fact pregnant, the baby could either be her father's or her brother's. She had let me take over control of her mind again before her brother did that gross thing to her. It wasn't nearly as bad as when her father did that stuff. What she had really been afraid of that night was having to watch Caroline go through anything bad. It had been a good thing that she didn't know everything that happened in that room.

CHAPTER THIRTY-FOUR

While I was alone once again washing the dishes I heard the no good intentions in my father's heavy footsteps as he entered the house. Again, as always, that awful feeling of fear crawled in and took hold in the pit of my stomach. I was washing the butcher knife and Julie suggested that I take my time with it. "Maybe if he sees you have the knife he'll leave you alone. Maybe you can use it if you have to." Would I? My heart was racing even faster than the thoughts in my mind. My head felt like it would burst from the pressure that was building up there.

He came closer. I could smell his breakfast still on his breath. "Hey. Why don't you leave the dishes to soak for now? I need you to come do something in the cel..." He had grabbed my arm and I didn't even have time to think.

I heard Julie from behind me screaming, "Do it! Do it now,"

and I knew what I had to do. And I couldn't screw it up or I would be dead. For real. I plunged that huge knife as deep up under his ribs as I could and lifted. It felt as if I had done as much tearing as cutting. If he had a heart I had to have hit it. Or some important inside part. I had to hold the knife tightly so it wouldn't slip out of my hands because it was wet and soapy.

"You monster! No more! No more ever again!" I shoved the weapon even deeper as I pushed away from him, praying to God that he was too hurt to fight back.

He stumbled back against the counter, sending a couple of the dishes I had just washed crashing to the floor as he grabbed for the knife that was still stuck in his chest. I had almost expected some sort of a black oil to come oozing out of the wound and was a little surprised when I saw the red blood. He had a look of pure shock on his quickly paling face. He opened his mouth as if to say something, but the only thing that managed to come out was more of his blood.

As if in a trance, I watched as the life drained from him. I listened as it came choking and sputtering from his mouth. I was the only one around to watch the death of our family's tormenter. "Good bye and good riddance John A For Asshole Fleischer," Julie said from my mouth.

I didn't realize until I heard the vomiting that my mother had also been watching. How much did she see? Whether she came in at the beginning or the very end, the scene pretty much spoke for itself.

She began to mutter something that I couldn't understand and then sat down right there on the worn throw rug on our floor, holding her knees to her chest, and began to rock. I left her there between the living room and kitchen by herself to mourn. Or to do whatever it was that she was doing. It was actually quite a sight to see someone as chunky as her huddled together in such a way.

I had a lot of work to get done. "Come on, Dad. We have a date in the cellar, remember?" I dragged him backwards, holding him under his arms. He was heavy, that was for sure. Luckily the stairs that led to where I planned to take his body weren't far. Once at the top of the staircase, I pushed my load so that it would fall down the rest of the way. Actually, Dad's body did more tumbling than falling. His body landed in a crumpled heap at the bottom. That was good enough for right now.

I turned back to the mess I had made in the kitchen. Ugh, I was quickly becoming exhausted and there was so much left to be done. I had to get busy. The other kids would only be gone for so long. I got out the stuff my father used to clean up the real messes and got to work. Luckily there wasn't a lot of blood, but there was enough. I scrubbed and scrubbed.

My mother just continued to sit there, rocking and muttering. "Hey, why don't you give me a hand here instead of just sitting there? Mom? This is your fault too, you know. You weren't even half this upset when Eric was murdered by Dad and you know that's what happened." No response. Just more of the rocking and the muttering. No worries. This part of the deed was almost complete. I didn't bother cleaning the butcher knife just yet. I brought that with me downstairs.

Julie took over from there. She told me I had done well and to just have a seat at the stairs in case anyone tried to come down. What a lifesaver she had turned out to be after all. Yes, it felt a little nuts that my doll was talking to me and doing my dirty work for me, but I was well past caring about that by this point. She had helped relieve a huge amount of stress and pain and suffering from my life and I just felt exhausted and thankful for her help.

It seemed like forever until Julie was done butchering Dad's body, but finally she was. I took the bones and scraps that couldn't be used out to the pigs' trowel, hoping they made every nasty piece disappear.

Whew! I finally got rid of that beast for Emily! Well actually she had done it all by herself, just with a lot of urging from me. Now maybe things could start to go the way that they should around this place. Now I had to just come up with a story to tell Emily's brother and sister when they returned from town. Also, it would have to be a story that we could tell anyone that came nosing around.

CHAPTER THIRTY-FIVE

It was quite a while before Johnny and Caroline came back home from bringing the produce into town to sell. That seemed to make us a little more money than just selling it roadside in our own yard and had been one of my ideas actually. Dad had finally listened and sent Johnny in his truck with Caroline to try the idea out and see if it really worked. He would never find out the answer, but it would be useful for the rest of us to know for the future.

I had mom seated and positioned the best that I could get her in her chair at the table and dinner was almost finished. Johnny looked around seeming confused and then asked, "Where's Dad? I wanted to show him this catfish I bought at the fish market."

I took him aside where Mom and Caroline wouldn't hear and

told him, "He left us Johnny. Just told Mom he was done with us. Hopped in the driver's side of some red head's truck and just sped off."

I could see him trying to let that news sink in. "But that makes no sense."

"Well, that's what happened. Mom's not handling it that well, so try to keep quiet about it." And then louder so that I could be sure everyone would hear, "I made dinner. Something Dad took out this morning. It should be done."

I dished Johnny's bowl and then Caroline's. Then I got Mom's. I was too worn out to be hungry. I took a seat next to Mom and tucked a napkin into her shirt. "Are you going to feed yourself or do I need to do it?" Johnny and Caroline both looked at me in surprise, but kept quiet. There was no answer from our mother. So I picked up the spoon and started to feed her some of the broth from the stew.

She didn't swallow and just let it spill back out of her loose mouth. I let Julie slap her across the face. Not hard, just enough to send a message to wherever she was at in her head. "You have to eat Mother." As I fished some more broth from the bowl, I noticed a big finger hiding in among the vegetables. It looked like a pointer finger. Oops, hopefully I didn't overlook too much of that. The next spoonful she swallowed. Good. She did the same with most of the rest of the bowl.

When everyone had finished their suppers and taken their bowls to the sink I asked, "Did I do an alright job with making dinner?"

"That was good," said Caroline, my sweet little sister.

"Good. Don't ever forget what Dad always tells us: don't get too attached..."

Johnny looked directly at me as he finished my sentence for me, "...because it might be supper."

There was a lot to figure out and take care of if Emily and her brother and sister were going to make it look like they weren't on their own in this house. Which, even though their mother was there in body, her mind had certainly taken off to someplace far away.

Emily and Caroline would also have to keep up with their school work. Johnny was old enough now not to have to do the school work any longer. One of them would have to figure out how to do the paperwork for The State.

They would also have to figure out what bills there were and how to pay them. There was a lot, but I knew they would be able to handle it. They had handled far worse when their father was alive.

ABOUT THE AUTHOR

Wendi Starusnak is currently living her own version of Happily Ever After in Phoenix, New York with her husband, her children, her mother-in-law, and their little dog that thinks he's a person. She began writing as a small child and whenever the question of what she wanted to be when she grew up was asked, she responded with, "a published author". She's hoping the fact that you're reading this now doesn't mean that she has actually grown up, only that her dreams have become a reality.

HOW TO CONNECT

www.facebook.com/AuthorWendiStarusnak
www.willowtree.b-town.us
On Twitter as Wendi Starusnak